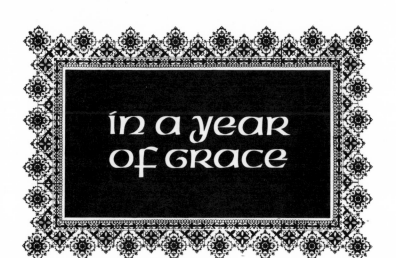

in a year of grace

HONOR TRACY

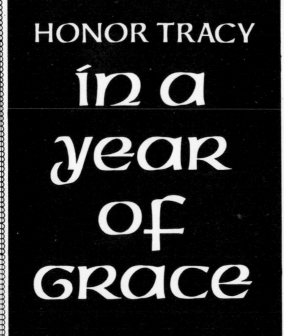

in a
year
of
grace

RANDOM HOUSE
NEW YORK

Library of Congress Cataloging in Publication Data

Tracy, Honor Lilbush Wingfield, 1915–
In a year of grace.

I. Title.
PZ4.T7621n3   [PR6070.R25]   823' .9'14   74–29595
ISBN 0–394–49506–3

Foreword to the American edition

It has been pointed out that there are certain Irishisms in the following book which may not be understood by the American reader, and these short notes of explanation are offered accordingly.

A bowsie man is a familiar figure in rural Ireland: he owns perhaps an acre or so of his own, does odd jobs for other people, is normally dressed in clothes that someone gave him, and is pretty wild to look at. Bowsie, the dictionary says, derives from bouzy = boozy = prone to drink, and this may or may not be the case.

The Gaeltacht is the name for those few enclaves in Ireland where Irish is still spoken as the ordinary language.

The Dáil corresponds to America's House of Representatives: it is the 'lower' but in fact decision-making house as against the endorsing Senate.

Garda is the Irish name for a policeman; plural, Gardai.

The Taoiseach is the Prime Minister, or head of the Government. The President in Ireland is a kind of figurehead, comparable to the Queen of England.

EEC stands for European Economic Community, usually known as the Common Market.

'Gas' is a very Irish expression of approval: 'Ah, you're gas!' means 'You're a great one, you are' in the same sense of being amusing and good company.

A T.D. is a Deputy, chosen by ballot to represent a constituency in the Dáil.

The Pioneers are teetotallers, who sign a pledge to abstain from all drink 'to make up to our Lord for those who take too much.'

A 'doat,' usually spelt so in Ireland, is something or someone fit to be doted on.

Complan is a kind of milky complete-food gruel for invalids that comes in powdered form.

H.T.

in a year
of grace

one

It was absurd, grotesque. Here he was, a Minister of State in a sovereign power like the Irish Republic, a power brought into being by the heroism of countless generations, and he was afraid to walk out of his own office door. Yet such was the case, and why? Because a bowsie man from somewhere in the Gaeltacht, not even a constituent, was waiting for him to do so. The fellow had some grievance, or thought he had. He had been making a nuisance of himself all over Dublin, picketing here, sitting-in there, pacing up and down before the gates of the Dáil, where he brandished misspelt placards or hurled abuse at the people's elected. He rang politicians up in their own houses at any old hour of the night. Now he had fetched up at the Department of Social Adjustment, a great burly yoke with a west-Irish face, seemingly carved from wood, and bushy black brows over fierce blue eyes.

A Garda came down the street, inspecting the parked and double-parked motorcars, sparing those that belonged to the important or influential, leaving tickets on others. The Minister thought of sending him word to see the intruder off. It was not violence he feared, but ridicule. There might be a scene, with a crowd springing up, one of those Dublin crowds that always range themselves on the side of a detrimental. It could get into the papers, and although the Minister would not have shrunk from the limelight as a general thing, this particular sort was not to his fancy. For God only knew what the reporters would say. With all those papers coming out and nothing much going on, they had to blow their material up, if only to fill the space.

He was about to ring for a messenger, when second and wiser thoughts prevailed. With a Garda involved, there was an even greater risk of publicity, and the affair would play into the hands of the opposition. On taking office, the Taoiseach had found himself with rather more loyal followers than jobs to reward them, and to meet this situation he had set up various, entirely new, departments. The measure, so bold, original and statesmanlike in the eyes of his party, had been greeted with howls of derision by your other men. All at once they realized, as they had failed to do when in office themselves, that the Republic was overloaded with Civil Servants already. Of its small professional or white-collar class, fully a third sat in Government offices, non-productive and under-employed, they pointed out: adding, how strange it was that the less officials had to do, the longer it always took them.

The Taoiseach answered all this with his usual spirit.

The departments were set up to cope with the needs of the new, vital, dynamic Ireland his party meant to create, a worthy member of EEC and its probable future leader. His party were not the ones to drag their feet, like a certain crowd he could name, not a hundred miles from where he stood. The new Ireland should find them equipped and prepared. It had been one of his election pledges to bring back the thousands and thousands of Irish exiles in England and provide them with jobs at home (catcalls here from the Opposition, who had given a similar pledge themselves) and it was their problems with which the new departments, notably that of Social Adjustment, would be called upon to deal. He spoke for an hour, with frequent interruption.

A question often put by the hostile was what, pending the new Ireland's creation, the Minister would do with himself all day: it was one that puzzled him too. He read the national papers for most of the morning, supplementing them with comics and racing news, but the afternoon lay heavy on his hands. And the ample staff his status required had to be occupied somehow as well. He got them to furnish reports on this and map out projects for that, but it was all curiously remote and insubstantial. He felt as if he were whirling round and round, like a cog that never engages.

Now he took his finger off the bell and went cautiously back to the window. The man was still below, haranguing the Garda and gesticulating towards the Department building. What on earth was to be done? Very soon it would be closing-time and the staff would leave, with himself stuck up in here like a tree'd cat.

He walked across to the bookshelves, swung open the front of handsome leather bindings and surveyed the bottles and glasses behind it. He had drunk two-thirds of a bottle of malt since lunch, apparently. With a shaky hand he poured the remaining third into a tumbler and took a swallow. The telephone shrilled, like a protesting guardian angel.

"Hullo? The Minister here."

"For Pete's sake, Brian, what's happened you? The guests are all arriving."

What guests were those, he wondered. Playing for time, "That you, Grainne?" he asked.

"Of course it's me. Who else?" She was yapping away like a hero. "Where are you? I expected you home an hour since."

Janey Mack! the garden party. For their daughter and her newly betrothed. The cream of Church and State to be there, or the rank and fashion of Dalkey anyhow. With a marquee and a brass band. Grainne all dolled up, and putting on airs. It had gone clean out of his mind.

"The country's business comes first," he told her gravely.

"The country's . . . You've been drinking." But the bite had gone from her voice, leaving only a weary acceptance of fact.

"Indeed then, I have not. I took a jar with me lunch . . ."

"You're jar'd altogether. Come on now and get home, d'you hear me? I can't handle all this by myself." There was a slam like a small explosion as the receiver went down.

It was to be hoped that no one had listened in. Brian hung up slowly and applied himself to the malt again. He was not drunk, *he* knew when he was drunk, none better; but he was certainly not at the height of his powers. Which was the more to be dreaded, the bowsie man in the street below or his wife, raging back there in Dalkey? His languid brain refused to make the choice. But when he had polished off the whisky and was fumbling with the cork of another bottle a brilliant notion struck him. There was no need to pass the bowsie man at all. He could climb down the fire escape at the rear of the building and follow a narrow passage between the two rows of houses which led into Bernadette Place. It was simplicity itself, once you'd thought of it.

Having drawn up this plan of action, he rang the bell and gave orders for his car to go round to Bernadette Place and await him there.

"I have decided to test the fire escape," he told his assistant. "Who knows when we mightn't need it?"

He thought that the young man looked amused, but could not be sure. There was some little delay in finding a key to the door that opened on the escape: there always was delay in finding anything whatsoever, and he determined to write a memo on this. As he stepped out on the iron platform, it trembled beneath him, as if it never had been designed for use; but it was too late to draw back now. Watched by the staff, he went gingerly crab-style down the swaying steps, wishing he'd braved the bowsie man after all. A nice fool he'd look, with his neck broken! but he reached the ground in time and, after fervently muttering thanks for his preservation, waved a jaunty hand at the craning heads above.

"We must get this lad fixed all right," he called up. "I wouldn't trust it under a cat."

Every face up there was stretched in a grin. He went his way, fired with a sense of achievement. Mick was before him in Bernadette Place, hunched at the wheel of the car, engrossed in the evening paper. He put it aside as the car door opened, but neither turned his head nor uttered a word. Every time they went out, the Minister was annoyed by the casual behaviour of his chauffeur. Surely it was Mick's place to leap from the car and, cap in hand, mind the door for him till he was in, asking, "Where to, Your Excellency?" Or, "Minister?" Even "Sir" would be better than nothing at all. But Mick merely sat there, wooden-faced, staring in front of him.

The Minister would have given his order now in a cool dignified tone implying rebuke, had he only known how. Instead, he heard himself say, with routine jocularity, "Home, Mick, and don't spare the horses." It always horri-fied Grainne, this familiar way of talking to servants, as she called them. Servants, how are you! She'd come a long way from the time when he knew her first, handing out the newspapers and smokes in her father's little shop down the country!

"Right you be," responded Mick.

The Minister leaned back and shut his eyes; but this made him giddy and he hurriedly opened them again, looking about for something on which they might focus. They came to rest on the driver's mirror, where he saw his face reflected, a heavy black smudge on the brow. For the life of him, he could not think how it had got there. Unless it was Ash Wednesday? He could not recall that it was.

"Is it Ash Wednesday today, Mick?"

"Ash Wednesday? It is not."

"But I seem to be marked with ashes, all the same."

"Today is the twenty-seventh of July," said Mick, in a voice that closed the inquiry.

Things were getting out of control. That last tumbler-ful, and the one before as well, had been an error of judge-ment. The stuff was working away inside, and the best would be, if he stopped talking altogether before he said something foolish. He took out a handkerchief, licked it and swabbed away at the smear, spreading it evenly over his forehead. Grainne was going to give out when she saw him. All through breakfast that morning she had been on, coaching him for her blessed party, what he was not to say and not to do. Even sober, he could never have come up to scratch and with things as they were, it would be plain bloody murder.

They were taking a long time to reach Dalkey. In fact, they seemed not to be on the Dalkey road at all. The car shot swiftly past open meadows and chestnut trees in flower, and there was a river snaking along with fishermen here and there on the banks. It must be, Mick was avoiding the jam that always built up round Blackrock at this hour of the day. The Minister felt pleased that he could still work things out so lucidly. But then Mick turned up a drive and brought the car to a halt in front of a spacious building with a brass-plate on the door. Nuns were peeping from the windows and two men in white doctor's coats stood on the steps outside, smoking and chatting.

"What's this at all, Mick?"

"Didn't you tell me, bring you home?"

So he had done. It showed you the state he was in. He never referred to his house as 'home' in the normal way but called it by its name of Capri Heights. Home was the facetious euphemism he employed for St Padraig and Collumcille, where he came for his dry-outs. And here he now was, at the other end of the world from Dalkey and a good hour's drive before he could get there. Holy Mother of God, he'd never touch another drop the longest day he lived . . .

One of the doctors had seen the Ministry car and was coming down towards it.

"Well, Brian my boy! Did we expect you this evening?"

"No . . . there's been . . ."

"Not to worry. No problem. I'll talk to Sister Lourdes. Hang on till I see."

He was gone before the Minister had sufficiently collected his thoughts. As he sat there, looking bemused, the other doctor approached to greet him in the same friendly spirit.

"Welcome back! Long time no see." It was in fact a bare six weeks since last he went in. "You've come at the right moment. A lot of the crowd are here, Kevin, Joe, Paddy, Niall, the pick of the nation. And a gas new lad from External Affairs. They're up in Mary Magdalene now, playing poker."

At last the Minister found the words he wanted. "I am not in any trouble today," he said with dignity.

"Of course you are not. Did anyone say you were? Come on out of that and I'll give you a hand. Take your time, now, easy does it."

The Minister got slowly out of the car and stood there, swaying a little and clutching his portfolio. The fresh air might clear his brain, perhaps, and help him straighten things out. Before this could happen, however, the doctor deftly shut the door and nodded to Mick, who at once set off like the wind. The Minister watched him go, wondering vaguely what it could mean. He felt somehow that he had lost control.

"Come on in and rest yourself," the doctor was coaxing. "Rest is what you need. You were working too hard."

The Minister approved his diagnosis. "That's true for you, anyway," he agreed. "We've a shocking amount on hands. If I'd known what the job would be like, I'd never have taken it on."

To bring out a speech of this length revived his self-confidence, and he began cautiously to mount the steps. It was good to be back at St Paddy's, with his friends before him inside. Thoughts of his wife and the party and the speech he was to have made now sank into some recess of his mind, to wait until called for. Sister Lourdes came tripping across the polished hall to receive him and say that his own little room was ready. Everyone here was pleasant and smiling, nobody scolded or made you feel inferior, passing remarks about the way you carried on.

Upstairs in his room they had unpacked the bag he always left there and laid his pyjamas out on the bed. They could hardly do more if you were Royalty. Fresh flowers in a vase, papers to look at, a little dish of holy water with sponge on the table beside his pillow. He got out of his clothes, leaving them on the floor, and into his pyjamas: slid between the sheets, dipped a finger in the holy water, blessed himself and fell soundly asleep.

two

The announcement of Nuala Hoolahan's betrothal to Dermot Wyllie was only a pretext for the garden party at Capri Heights. To begin with, Grainne was far from pleased by her daughter's choice. Had anyone told her eighteen years ago, at Nuala's christening, what that choice was to be, she would have been well content. The son of a well-known doctor, with a chain of creameries in the family— even if several times removed—would then have appeared as a catch. But since that day, when the pomps of the world were renounced on Nuala's behalf, things had taken up. Whatever the future might hold, at the worst the Hoolahans would always be of ex-ministerial rank. It was something that no one could ever deny. Surely, then, Nuala could have done a great deal better? And the boy himself, so odd, so unpredictable, so full of what he was going to achieve some day, so given to lying about at present . . .

"He's a very gifted writer," Grainne would explain when people asked: but if he happened to vex her, she would describe him to Nuala as "that reporter of yours."

Then Nuala would snap, "Hemingway started on news-papers too," and Grainne, without a notion of whom she meant, would grimly reply, "And so did Martin Maguire," a frustrated author, cousin of Brian, who had ended up in the London police.

The real idea behind it all was to prove, at a bound, by a single brilliant event, that Brian and she were able to hold their own with the cream of Dublin society. Hence, the preceding days were fraught with care, doubts and even anguish. She had never before entertained in such a manner, nor was she, as yet, at ease with the kind of people who would be there. She had met them, of course, while Brian was still a T.D., but in other people's houses, where nothing was expected of her. Now she had to take charge. Brian, needless to say, was no help at all, remarking, "I leave it to you," as his sole contribution. To ask advice fur-ther afield would be to give herself away, one of the dreads of her life; but on the other hand, what if the arrange-ments she made were inappropriate, unfashionable, not what the 'best people' looked for or, worst of all, ridicu-lous?

Everything seemed in conspiracy to undermine what lit-tle self-confidence she had. The catering was entrusted to a Dublin firm of long experience, patronized by all the lead-ing hostesses, so that here at least she felt sure of her ground. Yet she came away from her interview with the director, a suave Trinity College man, feeling that some-how or other she had merely amused him.

"I hand it all over to you, Mr Mansergh," she told him, with regal graciousness. "Only everything must be Irish, from the champagne down."

Mr Mansergh looked at her over his spectacles and replied, "I am afraid, Mrs Hoolahan, that Ireland produces no champagne as yet."

"I know that, of course," said Grainne, flustered. "What I meant to say was, Irish-bottled."

"I am sorry indeed to disappoint you," said Mr Mansergh, "but I fear that in this respect again we lag behind."

"Wasn't I hearing about some nuns in Carlow . . ."

Mr Mansergh closed his eyes for a moment or two, as if in prayer, before he answered. "Their product is non-alcoholic," he then disclosed. "Reverend Mother heard someone speaking of champagne and thought it sounded genteel. I can offer you a reliable brand, however, that is genuine Irish-imported."

"Well, that is better than nothing at all."

But she went away with an impression that he was laughing at her up his sleeve.

Then there was the matter of the invitation cards, their style and wording. She discussed it with Nuala, who first approved her ideas and then, once the cards were printed, found all kinds of fault with them. The patriotic border of gold and green looked, she said, as if they were pushing some product rather than issuing invitations, and the Irish harp embossed in gilt was too official, like something from the Post Office or the Revenue. The wording was wrong as well. It began, 'The Minister for Social Adjustment and Mrs Hoolahan request the pleasure of your company . . .' That would never do. Finally Grainne scrapped the lot and started afresh, renouncing colours in favour of black and white; but now her name was printed as 'Boolahan,' which, since time was moving on, had to be corrected in ink.

After this there was more planning, discussion, argument, reproaches, tears, hours of despondency, spells of bravado and constant appeals to the powers above. The Virgin was recruited, likewise St Jude, a novena made and another promised in the event of things going well. When at last the day arrived, Grainne got up and went to her duties blank and numb with apprehension.

But then the party began and all fell easily into place, so easily that she could not for the life of her think what the fuss had been about. The whole affair was amazing, if not indeed miraculous. Attendance had been one of the larger worries, the Irish guests having in the time-honoured tradition omitted to say whether or not they proposed to come. The single exception was Professor Wyllie, Dermot's father, who added to his formal regrets a cryptic personal note: "My wife thinks betrothal parties unlucky, and I can't leave the hospital that day. But count on us for the wedding!" which somehow had worried Grainne more than anything else. But here they were pouring in, Ministers, monsignori, tycoons, fashionable doctors and attorneys, and wives dressed in the height of Dublin *chic*.

Most of the men lost no time in separating themselves from their wives and moving in a body, slow but sure, towards the refreshment marquee. Even though waiters were bustling about with trays, they preferred to collect at the bar. It was a nasty plebeian habit, showing that whatever their eminence today they still were bogmen at heart; but Grainne could do nothing about it and there remained at least the clergy, a foreign diplomat or so and a sprinkling of Pioneers to leaven the female throng.

The defection of the Minister troubled her hardly at all. His blurry voice on the telephone had prepared her for it. He would only have put her to shame with his crude manners and vulgar repartee, and she much preferred telling people how sorry he was that urgent business had kept him away. Nor did the fact that Nuala had so far not shown up dismay her unduly. She had not expected anything else, for Nuala was always, everywhere, the last to arrive.

Capri Heights, formerly owned by gentry under a different name, was a commodious house in ample grounds which fell away in terraced lawns to a wood and thence to the shore. On the uppermost lawn was the marquee, large enough almost to contain the Dáil, and on the one below a brass band, lent by the Gardai, which from time to time played old Irish airs. There was not a cloud in the sky; and the vivid blue of Dublin Bay, the soft violet of the Wicklow hills, made a perfect setting for the animated scene in the garden.

All appeared to be enjoying themselves immensely. They took refreshments, chatted cosily, pointed out to each other the surrounding beauties, in the most civilized and upper-class way. Mrs Brophy, an American Embassy wife of Irish extraction, had brought her terrible child along, unasked, as she always did; but this was the only danger-spot and so far the little fright was quiescent, engrossed in ice-cream. The Press was there, sober to a man, and the steady click of their cameras seemed, more than anything else, to confirm the Hoolahan status.

Apart from this, moreover, Grainne was conscious of looking her best. She was one of those people who vary much in appearance. At home, shuffling about in apron and slippers, she could look like any old red-haired tinker, as Brian frequently pointed out. Nicely got up and feeling gay, she possessed considerable charm. Now she wore a dress of shimmering green and gold that suited her to perfection, and was of a highly elegant cut. Beside it, her fellow countrywomen looked dowdy and provincial. They had never outgrown their taste for garish colours and, en masse, formed a distracting mosaic of scarlet, purple, emerald and kingfisher blue. An experienced eye could tell at a glance precisely where in Grafton, Dawson or Wicklow Street each lady had done her shopping. But there was no tracking a garment such as Grainne had on: it simply was not Dublin, and received acclaim as grand, gorgeous, darling and a doat.

Inwardly preening, Grainne smiled the tributes off with an airy "This old thing!" or "Glad you like it!" But then the devil decided to take a hand: or so Grainne assumed, since, like so many of her people, she seldom connected misfortune with anything done by herself. He whispered to Peggy O'Rourke, who never shrank from direct inquiry, to ask in so many words where the garment came from, and put into Grainne's mouth the laughing reply, "Sure, I ran it up myself!"

The moment these words were uttered, she felt ready to sink into the ground. She had never made anything in her life. It was all she could do to sew on a button or mend a sock. The truth was not for telling, of course, but left alone she would have said it was the gift of some relation in New York. This was a clear case of diabolical intervention.

"Are you serious?" Peggy was screeching. "Hi, everyone, Grainne made the dress herself! Isn't she great?"

This brought all the women round her again, to marvel and cluck. To think of her fitting a dress like that all alone! How did she manage the back? Had she a row of eyes round her head, or was it done with mirrors? If it didn't beat all! There was no one in Paris to touch her, and wasn't she modest about it too? Never breathing a word till Peggy steam-rollered it out!

They laid it on so thick, it must be, they knew and were mocking her. On the fringe of the mob, Doreen Lehane was murmuring behind her hand to the redoubtable Eva Kelly, to whom you could hardly mention a soul but she recalled the grandmother walking barefoot on the roads, munching a crust of bread. Mme Duchêne, the French Counsellor's so voluble wife, raised her eyebrows and said nothing whatever. All was suddenly changed, as a pleasant dream turns to nightmare, by the devil's fiendish work.

But then St Jude, or even Our Lady Herself, entered the list in a brisk and businesslike fashion. From the lily pond rose a succession of piercing screams and Grainne sped towards them, thankful for the diversion. The Brophy brat had thrown herself in, to attract attention, and her mother was shrieking for help before she drowned. There was no question of that, for the water barely reached her waist as she sat among the lotus blooms and leered at the sky like a basking frog. Something of the sort occurred wherever she went.

"Does *nobody* have a lifebelt here?" Mrs Brophy was bawling.

"She couldn't drown in that if she tried," Grainne assured her, panting. "She's in the deepest part of it now."

Mrs Brophy calmed a little but was too worked up to subside altogether. "We-ell, say she gets pneumonia? She's all I've got. You should put railings around this pool before anyone else falls in."

"I didn't fall in," crowed Glorietta. "I jumped."

"I guess she got tired of standing around," Mrs Brophy went on in her carping way. "She likes to sing and dance in company, but nobody asked her here. How are we going to get her out?"

"She'd best walk out by herself," Grainne said. "Come on, there's the girleen."

"What'll I get if I do?" asked Glorietta, who bargained with a keenness beyond her years.

"Why, just anything you want, honey, if you'll only come at once," said the anxious mother. "We have to take you home and change those wet clothes."

"Okay, it's a deal." Glorietta struggled to her feet and

waded towards the bank, wisps of greenish slime clinging to her skirt and chubby legs.

"That dress cost me a hundred bucks," wailed Mrs Brophy, her thoughts changing direction. "This is only the second time she has worn it. I should have kept her in jeans."

"You like to show me off," said Glorietta pertly, baring her braced teeth as she clambered ashore. "I heard you telling Pop, there wouldn't be another kid to touch me."

She trotted off to the party, running from group to group and bragging of her exploit. Following, Mrs Brophy was just in time to overhear Lady Belling remark, it was a pity she had not stayed in the water for good, or better still, been drowned at birth. A lively exchange took place between the two ladies, provoking general amusement; and Grainne breathed again.

Her relief, however, was of short duration. No sooner had the Brophys left than a tardy guest appeared in the shape of Mrs Hogan, wife of the Minister's bank manager. Grainne received her graciously, with a certain consciousness of the difference in their standing; but when she began her set speech about Brian's urgent political duties, Mrs Hogan interrupted her with a weary laugh.

"Political duties, how are you!" she said. "There's no need to cover up with me, Grainne. Are the two of us not in the same boat?"

"What do you mean?" Grainne cried, in sudden terror.

"Isn't your husband up at St Paddy's, along with my Paddy? I'm just after coming away."

"O Sacred Heart, will you keep your voice down?" Grainne muttered, glancing wildly round her. "He can't be, Julia. I was 'phoning him at the Ministry just a little while since, and he said that business had him delayed."

"He was just landed at St Paddy's as I was leaving," Mrs Hogan affirmed, not without relish. "They were helping him up the stairs, the creature, for he hadn't a leg under him." There was some little exaggeration here, for Mrs Hogan had been riled by her hostess's fancy airs; but she was not a cruel woman and, seeing Grainne's distress, took pity on her. "Sure, and what harm? They'll dry him out and send him back in no time at all. Paddy's more often there than not."

"Let's go to the tent and get a drink ourselves," Grainne proposed, her voice dull with despair. Was it for this she had made the novena? There must be half a dozen or more of the women present with husbands in St Paddy's: the story of Brian and his affairs of State would fly round Dublin and make everyone laugh. "You can open a bottle of the Lanksong now," she said to the barman, with a poor attempt at the previous grand manner.

"What's that, then, Missus?" he asked, bewildered.

"That stuff there, with the wire on it," she snapped, pointing to the champagne. Missus instead of Madam, what was Lanson . . .

"I never opened one of them lads before," the barman confessed. "Look's more like a class of bomb. I'd be in dread."

"And you call yourself a sommeliure! I'll have something to say to Mr Mansergh."

She looked angrily round and caught sight of Dermot, Nuala's fiancé, a fair-haired boy of twenty with slanting blue eyes and flowing muttonchop whiskers. He wrote for the *Dublin Inquirer* and was dressed in his working clothes, faded torn blue jeans with tinsel stars strewn over the jacket and a vivid scarlet patch sewn into the crotch of the trousers. Partly by reason of this attire he stood out from the rest of the gathering, but he was noticeable too for an incessant fidgety snapping of his fingers. The paper believed him to be up at the Zoo, recording the progress of a newly born giraffe; but he had taken French leave, thinking all would be forgiven when he broke the sensational news of his engagement to a Minister's daughter. Time was passing on, however, and there was no sign of the fortunate girl.

"Dermot!" Grainne hailed him. "Come on over here and open this bottle for me, there's a good man."

"Is Nuala landed, then?" he asked in relief. The champagne was to have been held back until the engagement was formally announced.

"Indeed she is not. I don't know where she is. I didn't see her all day."

"She went to Belfast on the excursion."

"To Belfast!" echoed Grainne in stupefaction. A loud report as the cork shot out seemed weirdly appropriate. "What in the name of God could send her there?"

"She needed something," Dermot said, evasively, as he poured the wine. "And if she's not back yet, it must be, she missed the afternoon train. Then she'd hardly be home before eight at the earliest."

"And what did she need, that she couldn't get here? And why just today, of all days? Everyone will be gone by eight."

"I only know, she meant to catch the afternoon train. It was little enough she had to do."

"And what was that? You're keeping something back." Grainne was indeed worked up, when she talked thus freely in front of Julia Hogan. "I am asking you, what did she want in Belfast that she couldn't find here?"

A glint of mirth showed in Dermot's lazy blue eyes as he answered, "You'd have to ask herself, I suppose."

"Belfast is great for shopping, all the same," said Julia Hogan, in a chatty kind of way. "I often go on the excursion meself. Everything is so cheap. And the people are so friendly. Of course, you might get blown up."

At this, Grainne's thoughts took a new and terrible turn. It must be, something had happened. Nuala didn't miss the train at all. She was lying somewhere, in hospital or on the road, with maybe her legs blown off or her eyes out, or in pieces altogether and dead. Nuala, her own little baby girl, dead. Her mind swept on to the requiem mass, herself all in black, heavily veiled and weeping, and the Taoiseach there, and the President, and the television cameras. An address by some fashionable priest, and then the cruel yawning grave out there in Glasnevin, the coffin, so small, so light to carry, lowered in, earth falling upon it . . .

"Why don't you do something?" she shrieked at Dermot.

"And what could I do?"

"Ring someone up! Find out what happened! Aren't you a newspaperman?"

Her mind continued racing along with her own part in the drama. She saw herself, bowed with grief, breaking the news to the company, asking them please to forgive her and go. She was sure they would understand, she said, her voice choked with tears. In a respectful hush they took their departure, except for the newsmen, who fell upon her like so many vultures. She was appealing to them, in vain, as Irish gentlemen, when Nuala flounced into the marquee, looking thoroughly hot and cross, wearing jeans similar to those of Dermot, except that the crotch sported a patch of canary yellow.

Relief, as so often, took the form of rage. Grainne burst into furious reproaches, of which Nuala took no notice whatever.

"Give me a drink, barman, do," she said. "And a real one, not that stuff."

"A ball of malt," suggested the barman, with a happy sense of returning to his element.

"Fine." She drank the whisky off at a gulp and held out the glass for more.

"Don't stand there sousing. Go and get dressed. What kept you all the while? Dermot says you were in Belfast.

Then why weren't you back two hours ago? I thought something had happened you."

"Something did," Nuala snapped, between her swallows.

"What then? Tell me that."

"Barman, when you're ready," Nuala said, ignoring her mother and holding out her glass again. "I'll have another and then lie down. No party for me, I'm destroyed."

"But the whole thing is for you and Dermot," Grainne stormed. In the need to focus her wrath on some object, she forgot her social aspirations. "There I was, working my fingers to the bone!"

"No one asked you to," Nuala retorted, with truth. "It was your idea, not ours."

"Fine thanks, for all my trouble!" But there was no arguing with the girl when she was in one of her moods. "Well, what was it that happened to you? I insist on hearing that much."

"I am tired out and going up to bed," Nuala replied, emptying her glass and putting it down. "Are you coming or staying, Dermot?"

"Coming."

The two of them hastened indoors together.

"Honest to God, the young these days!" lamented the mother. She had thrown in the towel now, and was speaking to Julia as woman to woman. " 'Barman, when you're ready'! You'd say she spent her life in a pub. And telling Dermot she was off to bed, and was he coming with her! What kind of talk is that, and from a pupil of Bambino Gesú?" For such was the name of the exclusive convent that Nuala had attended.

"Ah, she'll never take off her clothes," opined Mrs Hogan sagely. "Something happened up North to upset her, and she wants a bit of consoling."

"And need she get into her bed for it? And what can it have been? Suppose she was in a fight with the soldiers: it would be on the papers. Brian would eat her—you don't know where you are these days."

It was a fact. Mere trifles were splashed all over the place, if they had to do with a Minister or his family, such were the drawbacks of prominence. Discretion was used in the matter of St Paddy's, because once you started on that no one could say where the end would be, and because most of the papers were represented there themselves; but that was the sole tabu, and the only crumb of comfort.

Poor Grainne was on the verge of tears. The afternoon was in ruins. Everything had fallen apart. What had she done to deserve all this? She looked dismally round the scene before her, at the men laughing and shouting and calling for drinks as if they were at home or in a public house, many of them half-seas over, none paying her the slightest attention. With the smell of drink and tobacco, the hot red faces, the shattering guffaws, it was like the liquor tent at a race-meeting. After all her dreams and hopes, these vulgar men were dragging her party down to the brutish point where they felt at ease. Most likely some would finish up on the ground, asleep or unconscious.

"Well, let's go back to the others," she said; and then, with a brave attempt at a smile, "there's one thing in it— nothing else can happen now!"

But in this she was sadly mistaken.

As Julia and she emerged from the marquee together, Mrs Grieve the Rector's wife was belatedly arriving. All that Grainne could see of her as she threaded her way through the crowd was a large pink face under a ludicrous hat; but for some reason her appearance was creating a remarkable stir. People looked at her and then at each other: titters rose in her wake and smiling comments were exchanged on every side. When at last she reached her hostess and Grainne saw what was up, she felt positively faint: for

Mrs Grieve was dressed in the very same model as herself, with the very same colour and stuff.

Unaware of the sensation she was causing, Mrs Grieve began to apologise for her lateness, due, she said, to a particularly frenzied meeting of the Mothers' Union. But then all at once she broke off and burst into her loud jolly laugh. A stranger to embarrassment, she pronounced in a ringing voice the terrible words: "So you read the *Sunday Times* as well!"

It was indeed in that publication that Grainne had found the Special Offer to readers, from a firm of dress-makers-by-post. She had filled in the form, received the patterns, made her choice, sent off her measurements and cheque. It was something the wife of an Irish Minister, committed to buying Irish, should never have done; but her tracks had been carefully concealed. She had the garment posted to a confederate in Liverpool, who reparcelled it in anonymous wrappings, described it on the customs label as 'Used Clothing' and for extra safety added the words *Erin go bragh*! with a flourish. It had slid through the customs office as if buttered. And now, by a cruel thousand-to-one chance, she was doubly exposed, first as a liar and then, far more heinous, as a reader of English newspapers and a patron of English industry.

"Those people make most of my frocks," Mrs Grieve was confiding at the top of her lungs. "And charge a third of what you'd pay here. But what a lark, our picking the very same one! Actually, it was the Rector's doing. I liked the model they called Miranda, but he thought it rather too flashy."

"Let me offer you something to drink," Grainne mumbled, steering her guest towards the marquee before she made any further disclosures. This was what came of mixing with Protestants. At least, the topers collected in that roomy canvas shelter would never notice or care what a woman had on her back; and indeed the curious sight of them both, uniformly arrayed like a pair of improbable twins, made no impression at all.

Mrs Grieve, for her part, could not cease chuckling over the splendid joke as she sipped her wine. It was all Grainne could do to be civil. Worries of a practical nature tormented her at the same time. Clearly, her wisest plan was to deluge the party outside with champagne; but the barman's dread of the bottles could not be overcome, and was shared by the waiters. One of the volunteers for the task, a guest, dropped a bottle or two and soaked all in the vicinity with such as he managed to open, until Grainne finally took the job on herself. By the time she had done and the waiters sped forth with their trays, she felt on the verge of collapse.

"Yours is a better fit than mine," Mrs Grieve was trumpeting now. "But that was my doing. When I sent in the measurements, I was looking ahead. There's a wonderful diet of milk and hard-boiled eggs that takes off a couple of pounds a day. I'll be as thin as a dog in no time at all!"

At this a number of dignitaries of the realm standing by burst into raucous laughter. One of them said something about fading away, another made a reference, clearly audible, to the hippopotamus. Grainne looked at them, all reduced by drink to the same mindless level, with weary disgust. The band, which had been silent awhile, struck up again with something cheery and vulgar, like a tune from a musical comedy or perhaps a boating song. What were they about? This was no sweet traditional air. Then she realized with a shock that it was the national anthem. She herself had told the band to play it when they reached the end of their programme, as a graceful hint that the party was over. There could be no more skulking in the marquee. The Gardai had to be thanked for their services and refreshed, and the departing guests seen off. Somehow or other she must find the nerve to sally out and face all those derisive glances.

"Don't stir," she said dully to Mrs Grieve, for to reappear with her side by side was beyond her powers of endurance. "Please look after yourself, while I see how things are going out there."

"I love champagne," roared Mrs Grieve, seizing the bottle, "but of course we can't afford it."

On one point Grainne, leaving her refuge, was quite determined. There would be no second novena made. If the powers above were looking for one, let them whistle for it.

three

On Nuala's admission that something had happened, Grainne assumed at once that whatever it was had taken place in Belfast. Julia Hogan had done the same and, as soon as Grainne and Mrs Grieve were out of sight, she lost no time in passing on her views to the company at large. Having no information to go on, she could speak the more freely; and she gave it unhesitatingly as her opinion that the girl had been involved in some perilous secret mission.

"Her grandpa all over again!" she cried in admiration—that gentleman's many years in Wormwood Scrubbs had laid the foundations of Brian's political career—"I declare, she's nothing less than a female Joan of Arc!"

All who heard her accepted this view and also took it for granted that Nuala had been, in some sort, a victim. Where the North was concerned, or when it was even mentioned, everyone stopped thinking altogether and merely reacted, much as a leg jumps at a tap below the knee.

In fact the visit there had passed off smoothly. Nuala bought what she wanted and then went for a snack with a friend in one of the few decent bars left standing. The city itself was quiet that day, an explosion or two, various fires, the occasional crack of a rifle . . . She caught the afternoon train and travelled home to the Republic, as so often before, without the least misgiving.

In the long open compartment there was the usual sprinkling of housewives, lured North at the risk of life and limb by the better and cheaper shopping, their bags and holdalls stuffed with booty. Children threw orange peel on the floor or spilled Coke on the tables, with their national gift for creating instant slum wherever they happened to be. A seedy middle-aged man distributed cards here and there, with questions on them about the purpose of travel, the length of stay and similar matters of no imaginable interest. Presently he collected them up again, filled in or not, and thanked the people for their cooperation. In a word, the journey today passed off exactly as always.

But when the train stopped at Connolly station, Nuala saw at once that something was afoot. There were extra Customs men on duty, and a number of uniformed Guards. Further along the platform, beyond the barrier, a group of women waited with a purposeful air, some with banners and streamers in their hands which at present they were keeping furled. It was clear that a demo of some kind was about to begin. Now from the next compartment another group of women got down and hurried to the Customs counter ahead of everyone else. These were no Dublin housewives, but a motley crew of wild appearance, some with the trailing skirts and matted hair of hippies, others in soiled jeans, most of them young and all in truculent mood.

Having lined up facing the Customs officials, each produced a packet and flourished it in the air, shouting, For Sale! For Sale! while some of the women outside ran forward, brandishing pound notes. At the same time those with the banners and streamers shook them out and raised them aloft, bawling the slogans on them at the top of their lungs. This is Woman's affair! they yelled. Priests hold forth, Woman brings forth! We want the Pill, and get it we will! and other impious cries of a similar trend.

Despite the warm sunny day, Nuala felt cold and numb with horror. It must be those frights from Women's Lib. Dead to all shame, with no decency, religion or fear of God, they were always drawing attention to themselves and getting their names in the papers. Involving respectable people too, they couldn't care less. And the things they were shouting, things you'd hardly mention between four walls to your closest friend! Where was the sense of it? Why could they not arrange things quietly and reasonably, as Christians should?

The Customs officers were demanding the surrender of the packets. The owners all refused, and broke out in the same dreadful clamour as their sympathizers beyond. Now the Guards were moving in, and Nuala was seized with panic. She could not think what to do, for pass the Customs she must, and with this scandalous carry-on all females were bound to be searched and involved, no matter how innocent they might be. Like a trapped animal, she threw desperate glances all around. Immediately behind her stood a man with a pleasant fatherly look about him, who seemed more amused than shocked by all the commotion. On a sudden impulse, she drew a little packet out of her handbag and said to him urgently under her breath:

"Would you ever take this for me, till I'm through? Or I'll be stuck."

"Sure," said the man with an understanding wink.

O blessed Irish sympathy with all in trouble! But it had been a fearfully narrow escape. When it came to her turn at the Customs desk, her hands shook so that she could hardly unfasten the bag again. Noting her agitation, the officer fumbled in every corner of it and finally turned it upside down, scattering its contents on the bench. Then he leaned forward and felt the pockets of her pants, skin-tight as they were, affording no place of concealment.

"So you've nothing at all to declare?" he finally asked, reluctant to let her go.

"Nothing at all," Nuala said, gathering up her possessions and looking annoyed.

"Only this," said the pleasant fatherly man; and he handed her parcel over the counter.

The official tore the wrapping off and studied the contents with satisfaction. "Nice work, Jim," he said. "This is contraband, miss . . . ma'am . . . as you very well know. You'll have to leave it after you, and give me your name and address."

Had Nuala been a little older, more self-possessed, adroit and knowledgeable, she might have talked herself out of this dilemma. Disclaiming any connection with the demo or plan to offer the goods for sale, she could have referred to a Supreme Court ruling in the past, to various bills before the Dáil at one time and another and to different groups and societies concerned with this very question; and so confusing a display of erudition, coupled with the fact that Irish officials seldom know what their regulations are and only wish to live in peace, would almost certainly have carried her through. But she was eighteen, ignorant, insecure outside her family circle, and she had never been in a tight place before; and she completely lost her head.

"That's not mine," she snapped. "I never saw it till now."

"Go 'way." said the Customs man. "Now, if you're ready!" and he took out a notebook.

There was nothing else for it. The horrible act of treachery had left her without a leg to stand on. Sulkily, she gave her name as Patsy Moran, with an address in Orwell Road.

"That's the Redemption Fathers," her betrayer said, wagging a finger at her in fatherly fashion. "Tut tut tut!"

"You're nothing but a bloody spy!" shouted Nuala.

"I'm a detective, really," he informed her, unmoved. "I'll take her in so, Michael, along with the others. There'll be quite a few, be the looks of it."

In fact, the demo having declined to leave, a number of arrests were made among them and the turbulent smugglers pulled in also. Nuala presently found herself in a van with these, en route for the Bridewell.

"And you told them there who you were?" Dermot marvelled, at this point of the narrative.

"Sure, what else could I do? They could have kept me in for the night. All the others refused and they put them in cells. They looked embarrassed, I can tell you that. They'd probably have let me go at Connolly. Down at the Bridewell it was too late. And now I suppose they will prosecute me."

"Ah, they will not. Your father will fix it." Dermot's cynicism was partly professional, partly innate. "I doubt they'd even try to, though. It might get into the English papers, and that wouldn't look well."

"And what will Daddy say to me? He'll be raging. And Mummy will be worse. When it comes to things like that, they're hardly sane."

"They must know, times are changing."

"Indeed then, they do not. Only last week Daddy had a blazing row with one of his oldest friends, just for saying that birth control would have to come. And we're not even married! They'll eat me!"

"You'll tell them the stuff was planted on you, and stick to that," Dermot directed. "They'll be glad enough to believe you."

"But there was that brute of a detective! And looking so decent, too. There isn't a soul to be trusted these days."

"It's only his word against yours, if it ever gets as far," Dermot pointed out. "And who's going to believe a cop?"

"But who would have dreamed of such a thing? In Ireland?"

"You would go with the excursion. That was a false economy. If a demo was planned, it was sure to be on excursion day, with a crowd of people looking on."

"Those creatures from Women's Lib!" Nuala said, with disgust. "Making a show of themselves, yelling and kicking. One of them bit a Garda on the thumb. And the language in the van . . . I declare to you, I'm ashamed of my sex."

"Why so? If they bawl long enough and loud enough, they'll get what they want. Then you won't have to go sneaking up North again. Come on, forget it, and give me a kiss," said Dermot, snuggling down in the bed and pulling her to him. "And no more guff."

"But we haven't the . . ."

"Ah, don't mind it!" The jaunty strains of the Soldier's Song floated up from the garden beneath. "Now! the party's breaking up. Not a moment to lose."

After an interval Grainne appeared and, to her relief, found them fully clothed and sitting demurely side by side on the sofa. They were sharing a reefer, puff and puff about, while the spicy fragrance wafted through the room; two innocents in a scented bower.

"What a gorgeous smell in here," she remarked, sinking on to the newly made and immaculate bed.

"We were burning a joss-stick," Dermot said. "Is the party over?"

"Thanks be to God."

"Will I give you a hand, clearing up, before I go back to work?"

"No, we'll leave it till later. I must get out of these shoes, they have me destroyed." She kicked the offenders off and contemplated her swollen feet with a frown.

Nuala was frowning too, but with disapproval of her mother's habits. It was a cause of tension in this rising family that the levels attained by its members varied so much. At the bottom was the Minister, paradoxically enough, as their rise in the world was entirely due to him. In speech, dress and manners, he continued as he had begun, unconscious that what suited a country auctioneer was out of place in a national leader. Grainne, on the other hand, by unremitting study and observation, had raised herself to the point where she could pass for an average suburban housewife; but it was merely a part she played, intended for onlookers, and once these were absent she thankfully reverted. Their children—nine to begin with but the Lord had taken three—had been given advantages denied to themselves, each one more as the parents' prosperity grew, until Nuala the youngest was quite the lady, and inclined to turn up her nose at all the others.

"Didn't I hear them playing the Soldier's Song a while ago?" she now inquired, in a mood for trailing her coat. "Whose corny idea was that?"

Grainne was up in arms at once. To have the republican anthem played had struck her as a charming and dignified gesture, even if, when it came to the point, things rather misfired. People felt awkward, standing to attention with glasses in their hands, and Lady Belling talked loudly through it, causing some little stir. Her ladyship was hardly to blame, having not the least idea of what the tune could be, but Grannie saw it as a deliberate affront, and several of the foreigners had looked distinctly amused.

"There's nothing corny about the Soldier's Song," she asserted, with a vehemence born of feeling none too sure, "and the national anthem's alway played at the end of a function."

"Not at a private party," Nuala said. "And we only play it at functions to copy the British. No other country does so."

"Will you stop!" Grainne cried.

"I'm telling the truth, amn't I, Dermot?"

"Well now," said Dermot, a precocious diplomat.

"We're always running the British down, yet we copy every blessed thing they do."

"Don't let's start on the British," Grainne appealed, in expiring tones. "I've troubles enough without them!"

"I was only saying," Nuala purred, well pleased with the effect of her words.

She had holed her mother's defences once again. Grainne was harrowed afresh by doubt and misgiving. Most likely the anthem had been a *faux pas*: whatever she did seemed to be wrong, particularly on the rare occasions when she felt certain it was right. She had, for example, asked Mrs Grieve from a sense of duty, in the ecumenical spirit, and look what came of that. Her very triumphs had a way of turning to ashes. She had been amazed and delighted when Lady Belling accepted the invitation, sent purely as a matter of form because the woman lived in the house next door. As a good Irish democrat, she abused and derided the former ascendancy for all she was worth, while secretly wishing it would take some notice of her. A titled woman among the guests was a feather in her cap, but then what happened, the creature barked away through the anthem, showing contempt for her hostess and for the Republic too! Such were the dismal thoughts for which she could thank Nuala, her own little girl, whose imagined

death and funeral had pierced her heart with sorrow barely an hour since!

"Well, this won't buy the baby a bonnet," said Dermot,
on whom danger signals were never lost and who was adept
at keeping out of harm's way. "Back to the grind for me."
And he made rapidly for the door.

"Keep an ear to the ground for you know what," Nuala
called after him, with a conspiratorial air. "And mind
now, never a word to a soul!"

"About what? What now? What is all this mystery?"
Grainne rose to the bait as she always did.

"Ah, it's nothing. If you'll excuse me, I think I'll go for
a bit of a swim. It was hot enough all day."

As Nuala moved about the room collecting her things,
Grainne was vaguely aware of something odd in her appearance: odder than usual, that was, for she could never
get used to the young and their unisex apparel. Something
was definitely strange or different or out of place but, weary as she was, she could not immediately pin it down.
Only when Nuala had gone, did she realize that the
diamond-shaped inset in her crotch was of a flaunting scarlet.
Surely—or was she mad?—it had been of a conspicuous yellow?

four

Dermot had lively powers of imagination, but with a peculiarity in them which hindered their being used to the best advantage. He felt cut out to be a distinguished author and rather carried himself as if this were already the case; but when he sat down to a pile of virgin foolscap, sharpened pencil in hand, to begin a novel or play, these powers promptly went to sleep. Either he found nothing whatever to say—the usual outcome—or what he did find was flat, ponderous, a faint echo of work by somebody else. But let him engage in the more humdrum business of reporting an actual event, and these same powers immediately sprang to life. Then the wings of fancy bore him aloft to such purpose that those who had witnessed the event themselves would often fail to identify it from his description.

So vigorous were these wings, indeed, that he could report most vividly on scenes and occasions at which he had not been present. Creation from the void might be beyond him, but let there be a single solid fact in being, a ceremony, a race, an accident, and he could bring it all to life without leaving his bed. For this reason, while disappointed at not being able to announce his engagement to Nuala —which in his young vanity he had thought of as front-page news—he was not in the least perturbed about the baby giraffe. On reaching his office, he at once sat down and wrote a touching account of the little creature, unsteady as yet on thin graceful legs, nuzzling his proud affectionate mother and looking out at the strange new world about him with sparkling river-brown eyes. He wrote easily, without changing a word, signed the piece with a flourish and sent it round to the deputy editor, Seumas Duff.

The editor and his deputy were both in despondent mood. This was so frequent as really to constitute their normal condition, and arose quite simply from the lack of Irish news. All the national papers were in like predicament. For the honour of Ireland, they had to be as big as, and to cost somewhat more than, their English contemporaries; but then the problem posed itself, how on earth to fill up the space. They lacked the means for a wide foreign coverage, and even had there been one, the majority of readers would have skipped it. All they wanted was their own parish pump, but life around that pump was plodding, slow and uneventful. There was, to be sure, much that needed saying but on the whole it was left unsaid. It was this state of affairs that imparted to the national press so curious and distinctive a flavour. The verbosity, repetition, flogging of dead horses and the purple patches might appear to be the work of pedants or psychopaths: in fact, they resulted from the need to stretch over a page or more what should have gone into half a column. Then there was the deadening hold of myth, the eternal public declarations of what no one privately believed. All in all, the task was a thankless one, an empty grind to no purpose, its sole attraction a kind of seedy glamour. The livelier talents removed to London at the earliest opportunity, the rest consoled themselves with dreams and drink or an occasional bracing feud.

That was the position the whole year round; but in summer the scene was especially arid. Now the long vacation was about to begin, and the Dáil, the High Court and the University were closing or closed. Strings of people announced, in the Social and Personal Column, their impending departure on holiday. The priest who resolved the doubts and calmed the fears of correspondents had betaken himself to Rome. Nothing seemed to be happening at all. The national pilgrimage to Croagh Patrick was some way off, the Horse Show further still. There were no strikes or fires, and hardly a decent motorcar crash. The *Inquirer* was padded out day after day with photographs, of anglers smiling beside some monster fish they had caught, weddings of bank clerks and shopgirls, American tourists laying a wreath on something, young drop-outs asleep on the grass in St Stephens Green . . .

At this particular moment, the editor, Mr Magee, and Seumas Duff were frowning over some galleys that littered the editorial desk.

"Not a real bloody story in the lot so far," lamented Magee. "Cost of food, drink, tobacco, petrol, clothing and railway charges to rise. That's not what I call news. Provos to launch another offensive. I daresay. More silly kids blowing themselves up. Anyhow, readers are sick of the North.

Ireland will lead the New Europe, predicted Senator Malachy Rooney of Texas at a Chamber of Commerce luncheon today . . ."

There was a hurried knock on the door, and a youth burst in waving a news flash.

"What now? Outbreak of World War Three?" demanded the editor, seizing it. " 'Is this the Ireland I fought and died for, was the impassioned cry of Mr Fergus Kilbane, farmer, of Ballyhaunis, summoned for the nonpayment of rates'—for Pete's sake!" He rolled the paper into a ball and hurled it across the room. "Scappa!" he said to the youth, who retired with a crestfallen air. "Where's Dermot at all? He should have been back hours ago."

"Most likely he went on to another story," Seumas replied, blue-pencilling the Senator from Texas with gusto.

"Without ringing up for instructions? He's getting too big for his boots." The photograph of Mrs Magee and the children fell on its face as the editor banged his desk in exasperation. "I won't have reporters careering about the place, and the office without an idea where they've got to."

"He's a bright lad, all the same," Seumas observed, as he threw the remnants of the Senator aside and started work on the Provo offensive. But at this moment there was another knock at the door and another youth appeared, with a typescript which he placed before the deputy editor, whose tense features relaxed a little as he looked it over. "Now! this is from Dermot. I thought he wouldn't be wasting his time." Yet as he read, the expectant look on his face turned to one of mystification, of incredulity almost, until by the time he reached the end he was staring at the paper as if it were written in Arabic.

"What's wrong there? Let me see that," the editor commanded. As he devoured the article in his turn his purplish face grew darker and his bushy brows shot up and down. "Bright lad, eh? To be sure. Quite so. Take all that rubbish out of here, Seumas, and do the best you can with it. And send Dermot to me at once."

Hunched over his desk, he sat and waited. Dermot came in, with the modest air of one about to receive a well-earned tribute.

"Sit down," Magee said gently, his tone oddly at variance with the colour, alarming by now, of his complexion. "I was reading this story of yours. A delightful piece of work."

"Thank you, sir," said the gratified author, coyly looking down.

"Fond of animals, I daresay?"

"Oh very, sir, very."

"Yes, I felt that. The only snag in your masterpiece is," Magee went on, and now a snarl like that of a hungry tiger crept into his voice, "that you were hardly out of the place on your way to the Zoo when they rang up to tell us the baby giraffe was dead."

A silence followed. Dermot could think of nothing to say. The editor could think of a dozen things and more, but was unable immediately to choose between them. Slowly and deliberately, to give himself time to make the selection, he lit a cigar and puffed a cloud of smoke in Dermot's way with every appearance of wishing it were poison gas.

"Shining river-brown eyes, eh?" he enunciated after a while. "Peering out at a strange new world. Tottering on slender little legs. Nuzzled by the proud and loving Mammy."

He released another bank of gas towards the culprit who. even *in extremis*, was wincing at the liberties taken with his prose.

"I suppose you know what this means?" barked Magee.

Dermot supposed he knew but too well. Look at poor decent Maguire, the Minister's cousin, once the respected drama critic of the *Irish Globe* and now a London cop, all through a sensitive appraisal, composed in the warmth and comfort of Durgan's snug, of *An Evening with Samuel Beckett,* capriciously and at the last moment cancelled. But how unfair, if he were to undergo a similar fate! Maguire's notice had appeared and set all Dublin laughing: his own lapse need never pass the four walls of the editorial office. And those four walls had, in their time, been the silent witnesses of matters infinitely more . . .

This train of thought was interrupted by the editor's voice. "Have you anything to say?" it was inquiring, but with a sinister intonation which implied that the question was purely formal.

Suddenly Dermot saw the way out, clear before him. It was not an admirable or elegant way: rather, it was the expedient of a drowning man who, seeing a smaller than himself on a raft, knocks him off and clambers aboard; but it was the only discernible one.

"Sir," he said, looking his employer full and frankly in the eye, "please let me tell you everything. Hear me out, and I believe you will not judge me too harshly."

"Fire away." The tone was brusque, but the clouds of smoke eased off.

"I was on my way to the Zoo," Dermot narrated, "when I got a tip-off there might be a biggish story at Connolly Station. I reckoned the baby giraffe could wait, but that this could not. My intention was to cover it first and go on to the Zoo after. But the story was even bigger than I had been led to expect, and it took so long and brought me so far afield, I saw there would be no time for the Zoo if I was to make the first edition. And so I rushed back to the office—only, as I began to write, to realize that I had been carried away, that the Connolly Station affair would never do, that the sensation, the scandal, would have our readers, nay the country itself, up in arms. Accordingly, sir, I must confess, having seen many a baby giraffe in my time, I did compose that little piece from my recollections of their habits, thinking it better than nothing."

Magee had heard the confession out, as requested, but with growing impatience, the cigar smoke shooting up in rapid short bursts like some urgent Indian signal. As soon as Dermot had done he exploded: "But the story? what story? Why does no one tell me anything? Am I the editor, or am I the doorman?"

"I hardly like to repeat it, sir," Dermot replied, demurely examining his fingernails.

"This isn't a convent, as far as I know," snapped Magee. "Out with it, boy, we haven't all night."

There was no help for it; and Dermot gave him a full account of the doings at Connolly Station and subsequently, as related by Nuala, but with various lively addenda of his own, such as a keen and practised observer would supply. Magee listened avidly and, when the recital was over, leaned back in his chair and surveyed the youth with something like affection. "A biggish story!" he chuckled. "Three columns or I'm a Dutchman!"

From the church next door a bell chimed out sharp and clear, drowning Dermot's gasp of horror.

"The Angelus!" cried Magee, hurriedly crossing himself. "Not a moment to lose! Hurry on, Dermot, and get it all down. This is your finest break yet!"

Dermot had a peculiar visceral sensation as if he were in a lift, dropping twenty floors at once. He had expected a sharp rebuke for his error of judgement, a warning to have better sense in future; and here was Magee, benevolence itself, preparing to splash the news all over the front page!

"I'd much rather you left me out, sir," he said faintly.

"I don't doubt it," was the jovial reply. "Everyone wants to be left out of everything, unless it's a round of drinks. Go on, Dermot, and give it all you've got. No one's going to shoot you."

Were they not! What would Nuala have to say, after swearing him to secrecy? She had inherited a temper from both sides of the family. And his mother-in-law to be, when she read his eye-witness account of carryings-on all over the city when he had been under her nose at Capri Heights the entire afternoon? She had no exalted opinion of him at the best of times. Back in his office, he fell into a chair and fumbled in his breast pocket for the box of reefers. It was empty, of course, he had shared the last one with Nuala herself. How often in life one came to regret a kindly unselfish deed!

He slid a sheet of paper into the typewriter and sat frowning at it, his mind a blank. The clock near by struck half-past six and then, it seemed almost directly afterwards, seven. Magee rang through, to ask how much longer he must wait. A vision rose in Dermot's mind, with galvanizing effect, of P. C. Maguire on his lonely beat in Shepherd's Bush. He began the story, lamely at first, then gathering momentum, until suddenly the artist in him came alive, took possession, and the words poured out of themselves, fresh, brilliant and graphic. By the time he had finished, misgiving and dread were gone, and his only thought was that here, beyond all question, was a masterpiece.

Magee was not in the habit of praising his staff, having found that to do so invariably led to a falling-off in their work or a request for higher pay, if not both together; but on this occasion he went so far as to mutter, "It's gas, young fellow, gas all right!" as he pored over the sparkling narrative. "Take this down to Seumas," he directed gleefully, when he had finished, "and tell him it's to lead."

A few minutes later Seumas appeared, with the typescript in his hand. He was looking sardonic, as the alternative to aggrieved, one or other of these expressions being habitual to him in the presence of his superior. Like many a second in command, he felt sure he would make a better first than the individual who actually was; and this feeling was exacerbated in his case by their being so nearly of an age that, short of some benevolent accident, there was little hope of his getting a chance to prove it.

"Are you serious, Editor?" he demanded. "Things like this don't happen in Ireland."

"It has happened," retorted Magee, cheerfully lighting a new cigar.

"You know what I mean."

Magee knew all too well what Seumas meant. Apart from a few cranks, subversives and publicity-mongers, nobody clamoured for birth control in Ireland because nobody wanted it. Joyfully they took whatever the Lord chose to send, 'peopling' as Fr Clapp, the *Inquirer's* religious correspondent, had so beautifully written a while ago, 'the Courts of Heaven.' This being the case, a demo such as was alleged to have taken place must be out of the question. He began to tidy the papers on his desk, a habit of his in moments of mental stress, as if by so doing he could arrange and marshal his ideas. His eyes fell on the photograph of Mrs Magee and the children lying face down, and he replaced it in its right position. His offspring numbered three, methodically spaced out, and with all respect to Fr Clapp there were not going to be any more; and something of the kind was true of many devout Catholics in his circle. In fact, the families of such tended mysteriously to be no bigger than those of heretics or pagans.

"All very fine, Seumas," he said at length. "But they can't hush it up. If those women were arrested, they will have to be charged."

"Then we report the proceedings, like any others, under privilege."

"And so does everyone else," argued Magee. "This is a scoop. I say, we'll go ahead."

45

"There'll be an almighty shindy. Have you forgotten, the girls getting abortions in England?"

"That was only because the Eucharistic Congress was on at Maynooth."

"Well, the new papal nuncio arrives tomorrow," was the glum rejoinder. "Something is always cropping up."

"So it's back to Forgotten Irish Patriots, I suppose, and The Gaeltacht is not a Museum," remarked the editor sourly.

All at once there was pandemonium on the floor below, which was at street level. Shouts were heard, followed by the tinkle of breaking glass: then the heavy front door slammed to and the shouting continued outside. Seumas hurried to the window and looked down.

"It's the nut," he reported. "The lad that's plaguing everyone about some injustice or other."

Magee had pricked up his ears when the noise began, like an old warhorse at the bugle call, but now he lapsed into gloom again. "No story there," he grunted. "We can't run grievances, unless they are national. Once we began on private ones, we'd be swamped."

There was another crash, as the intruder hurled a brick through the fanlight.

"Well, he seems to be doing a bit of damage, anyway," the editor commented, cheering up a little. "Go down and see if there's half a column in it. No injustices, mind. Unknown Assailant."

"Right you be," and Seumas departed on his errand.

Left to himself, Magee turned the business of the demo over in his mind. What had sounded perilously like common sense on Seumas's part now struck him as one more example of the fellow's chronic oppositionism. He was like the Old Lady who always said No. If matters were left to him, there would hardly be a paper at all.

Not only should the story appear and lead the paper,

but he would write a strong editorial himself. The difficulty was to decide on the line to take, whether of approval or denunciation. The younger doctors were becoming vocal on this question, urging the rights of the individual and pressing for a change in the law. A lobby existed already and could easily turn into a movement. On the other hand, the *Inquirer* could not abide Women's Lib and was traditionally inclined to be disturbed at the idea of women having any freedom at all.

Magee himself had no feelings one way or the other, in fact he was without strong convictions of any kind: decided preferences, say for Scotch rather than Irish whisky, was as near to them as he got. He sat for a while thoughtfully doodling and then, unable to make up his mind, concluded that the rational way out was to flip a coin. The die was cast for orthodoxy, and he went to work with a will, upholding the laws of God, Nature, the Vatican and the Irish Republic, castigating those who set themselves up in rebellion, under the very nose of Mrs Magee and her decently limited progeny. Then, throwing the piece in the printer's tray, he went to reward himself with a jar or two at Gogarty's round the corner.

five

St Padraig and Columcille in some ways was not unlike a prison. There were, of course, many and fundamental differences, apart from the comfort of the accommodation, the excellence of the food and the beauty of the grounds. The inmates were there of their own free will, by the persuasion of their families or at the insistence of their employers: they were paid for by themselves rather than by the community, and their relations with their guardians were almost invariably cordial. Nevertheless, as far as organization and classification went, there was a definite resemblance.

For example, one group of patients was kept in a wing

known as Top Security, more or less in complete isolation. Only very close relations, or colleagues bringing essential documents for signature, were permitted access to them, and these had first to open handbags or briefcases, and even at times to submit to frisking. They could never walk in the garden unaccompanied, lest some well-wisher beyond should lower bottles over the wall; and their outgoing mail was steamed open and carefully studied before being sent on, a practice made imperative by the ingenuity of the requests contained therein.

One man had a weekly crate of eggs delivered, which he kept in his room, saying there was nothing he loved better than to suck a raw egg now and then: whereas these eggs had all been carefully blown, filled with brandy and sealed with a minute blob of wax. It might never have come to light, had not Sister Lourdes, for some reason suddenly short of an egg, borrowed one and boiled it. Another miscreant received a beautiful azalea in an outsize plastic tub: no suspicions were aroused until one day, the patient being in his bath, kindly Sister Gracia noticed that the earth around the plant seemed dry and began to water it. Instead of seeping in, however, the water ran over the edge of the tub; and, looking more closely at the plant, the Sister found that it was not a real one at all, but a brilliant imitation. She next discovered that the earth was a mere inch deep, resting on a lid to which the plant was firmly attached: a vigorous pull on the stem brought the whole upward, exposing an underground lake of 78 proof rum.

"Isn't it a shocking thing, Father, they couldn't put the brains God gave them to a better use?" she lamented to the chaplain; and to the Senior Consultant: "You'd need eyes in the back of your head, blest if you wouldn't."

Nonetheless, the members of this group were able to graduate, when it was deemed safe, to the next. Surveillance here was strict as well, but there was free movement about the premises and grounds, association with other patients in the same category and visitors in the afternoon. Any attempt to pass the front gate, however—none but an acrobat or a mountaineer could have scaled the walls—was promptly thwarted by an attendant, springing up as if from the ground, who engaged the culprit in friendly conversation while escorting him back to the fold.

Finally, there were the provisional cures, corresponding to men on parole or ticket-of-leavers. Every morning they left St Paddy's and went about the nation's business, be it in State department, university, bank or Court of Law, returning only after work hours to continue their treatment out of harm's way. With the commencement of the holiday season many now were getting their full discharge, and their section was pervaded by a spirit of jollity, a kind of end-of-term feeling, all the pleasanter for the likelihood of their reassembling in the autumn.

It was in the second of these categories that, after careful thought, the Minister for Social Adjustment had been placed. Agreement on the matter had not been reached all at once. Some were in favour of Top Security, pointing out that poor Brian, in and out of the place for years, had become an ever more frequent visitor since his promotion. Others declared that, with so many of the staff on holiday, this was out of the question. Still others urged parole, to spare the family's feelings; but against this was argued that St Padraig's reputation had to be considered as well, and that it would not do for a so-called 'cure' to be reeling about at large, as Brian was on admission the night before. And so into Class B he went, happy to be with his many old friends and out of Grainne's reach.

At half-past three on the following day he was in his private room, sitting in an armchair and gazing out of the window. The modern techniques of the doctors, the loving care of the nuns, had not as yet begun to take effect. He felt depressed and irritable, at times even furious. His head ached, his eyeballs burned, there seemed to be a patch of molten lava at the base of his skull and his hands shook like those of an old man.

When Sister Lourdes came in to announce that he had a visitor, he all but exploded; and when she told him it was the Minister for Public Security, a man he disliked, he quite did so.

"I'm not fit to see anyone," he shouted. "What can the fellow want?"

"Didn't I tell him you were not at all well," Sister Lourdes replied. "But he's most insistent. It seems, he went all the way to your house first thing, looking for you. Come now! If he doesn't leave soon, just ring, and I'll say the doctor is here."

"Five minutes, then," grunted the patient, pressing a sponge of holy water against his brow.

The interview lasted much more than five minutes. To begin with, Brian was in no shape to follow what the man was trying to tell him, in the classy English accent that irritated him at the best of times. Ruairí na Rigg was the son of an English renegade, hanged for treason in the First World War, whose widow had brought up their boy to be more Irish than the Irish themselves; but he had never acquired their speech, as if sensing that humbug ought to have a limit somewhere. Certain other English habits clung to him also; for example, he had begun his narrative methodically at the beginning—with the publication of Dermot's article—to the utter confusion of Brian, who could not see what on earth it had to do with him or with anyone else.

"Women's Lib! Demos! What are you driving at?"

Patiently, Rigg went over the ground again. From the highest quarter the night before, the ukase had gone out that the whole affair was to be ignored, passed over, in fact had never taken place. Authority, religious and secular, was united in this decision. The women in custody had all been released. To the best of everyone's belief, only those directly concerned knew the first thing about it. And then the *Inquirer* erupted with its lavish front-page spread and scorching editorial. How the paper got hold of the story, no one could say, but concealment clearly was no longer feasible.

"And what's all this to me?" Brian fumed. "It's your department, not mine."

Ruairí na Rigg nervously cleared his throat. "That's what I'm coming to, Brian, if you'll only listen," he pleaded. "One of the young ladies implicated was a daughter of yours. Miss Nuala. And I'm very much afraid she will have to be charged."

Brian pressed the sponge on his forehead again until the holy water ran into his eyes.

"How implicated? Charged with what?" he asked angrily.

"Brian, that is what I am trying to tell you. With smuggling in contraband goods for sale. Contraceptives. And giving a false name to the Customs."

For a few moments Brian sat open-mouthed, while these words made their leisurely way through the fog in his brain. Then, with a roar, he sprang from his chair and seized the other man by the throat, with every intention of choking his life out. The noise of tables overturning and the victim's cries for help brought Sister Lourdes to the scene in a flash: she promptly set off the alarm installed in every room against such contretemps as these and two stalwart attendants as promptly answered it.

The terrified Ruairí was rescued by them and accompanied to his car by Sister Lourdes, all a-flutter with apologies. The patients would sometimes have these little spells when newly admitted, she said: they really amounted to nothing and were not to be taken personally. Mr Rigg, massaging his throat, replied that he was glad to hear it and drove away, quivering with distress and indignation. Sister Lourdes then hurried back to Brian, meaning to scold him well and hint that any repetition of such conduct might result in transfer to Top Security; but she found herself confronted with an entirely new situation. The fight had gone out of Brian, who sat slumped in his chair, covering his eyes with his hands, his shoulders heaving, while Reverend Mother stood beside him, outrage written all over her large red face, and stroked his head.

"Whatever induced you to let that fellow in, Sister?" she demanded fiercely. "It must be, he's out of his mind. There he sat, calmly telling Mr Hoolahan his daughter had smuggled contraceptives in from the Six Counties! and that she would be charged!"

"Jesus, Mary and Patrick!" gasped Sister Lourdes, turning pale and clutching the bedstead for support, while a sob burst from Brian.

"It's a wonder he got out of this alive," Mother Joseph proceeded in her grimmest tone. "God help us, the people these days! He could be made to pay thousands for the like of that. But what you'll please to tell me is, why did you let him in without asking his business? You should know the rules by now."

"I thought . . . a Minister . . ." quavered Sister Lourdes, still holding on to the bed.

"Ah, will you stop your nonsense? A Minister! Here in St Padraig's we only have visitors, and visitors are all alike." To this simple view of affairs, Reverend Mother had been led by experience. "Hurry on now, and help Mr Hoolahan into his bed. Then call Dr O'Toole and ask, would he advise sedation. And not a word of this to a soul, or we'll have a riot."

With that Mother Joseph swept from the room, with a flurry of skirts and a clatter of holy beads.

Sister Lourdes obeyed her orders to the letter, and Brian was shortly fast asleep, with a shot in the arm. Not even to Dr O'Toole himself did the nun confide the grounds of his disturbance; and yet, in some mysterious Irish way, the news got out, drifting through the sector until it reached his cronies in Mary Magdalene, and causing passionate resentment. The poker players threw their hands in, the chess addicts leaned back in their chairs, Kevin Magadoo the Justice hurled his book to the floor, and all joined in abuse of Ruairí na Rigg. Would you think a fellow could sink so low? He had some scheme of getting Brian's job for a friend, that was the long and short of it. Or some wicked spite against Brian himself, as decent a man as ever trod leather. Or wasn't it just the English blood coming out in him? You never could trust an Englishman, for all his father was hanged. One thing was sure: not a man of them would rest until he was driven from public life for ever.

Up at Capri Heights, meanwhile, Grainne was completely unaware of what had happened. Ruairí na Rigg had told her nothing except that he must see her husband on a matter of the first importance; and she was pleased and flattered by this, assuming it to be something to do with the State. It was mortifying to have to disclose to Ruairí, an abstemious man, Brian's present whereabouts; but he showed no disapproval, or even surprise, and simply made a pleasant allusion to her garden-party, of which he had read in the paper, before taking his leave. She easily dismissed his call from her mind and returned to her daily morning task of getting Nuala out of bed.

There was no reason for her to undertake this arduous and often impossible job. She did it because her mother had always done it to her; but then, in those days, she had to make the stirabout or wet the tea, milk the cow or feed the hens, before starting to help in the store. Nuala had no duties of any kind, and could sleep the whole clock round with no one a penny the worse. When she left her convent school the Christmas before, there had been a vague idea of her opening a boutique with a friend, one of those small noisy teen-age affairs that were forever starting up and collapsing again in Dublin now. But the plan was forgotten at once when she took up with Dermot, to the great relief of Grainne, who thought that ladies should not work. Despite all this, every morning found her at Nuala's bedside, urging her to be up and not lie there like a log, while Nuala grunted in her sleep, or turned on her other side, refusing to open an eye, with at the very most some mutter about 'ten minutes more.'

Nuala had profited by her mother's brief absence with Ruairí to slumber anew and was lying face down, her fists clenched on the pillow, in a manner which seemed to say that nothing less than a bomb would rouse her. Exasperated, Grainne went across to the basin to fill a sponge with cold water; but as she did so her eye fell on Nuala's clothing, scattered over the floor where she had dropped it, her briefs, her bra, her canvas shoes, the blue jean tunic with the tinsel stars, the tight pants with their scarlet inset in that most indecent location. And when she saw that, she stopped dead in her tracks, one foot raised like a pointing gun dog.

Yesterday evening she was near to exhaustion, her mind so full of her troubles and failures that she really felt sure of nothing. Now, restored by sleep, she knew that she had been right, that it had not been her imagination, that Nuala's inset had in truth been a canary yellow, Dermot's, the flaming red. What on earth could this portend? Did young couples exchange their trousers today, as formerly they exchanged rings, as a gage of plighted troth?

She took them up and felt in the pockets, hoping to

come on some final proof of ownership; but the contents, a book of matches, a grimy rag and the visiting card of one Abdul Hamid, were as unisex as the garment itself. Deeply puzzled, she was about to put them back when an exclamation from behind made her jump and spin round in confusion. Nuala, fully awake, was sitting bolt upright in her bed and looking intensely annoyed.

"What are you doing with my pants?" she demanded. "Why can't you leave things alone?"

"I was only tidying them up," her mother said lamely. "They were lying about on the floor. I'm sure you never flung your clothes about like this at the Bambino Gesú."

"Leave the Bambino Gesú out of it, will you? You were going through the pockets. Why?"

"The pants looked as if they could do with a wash and I was emptying the pockets before I took them away," Grainne said with her best martyred air, that of a loving but undervalued mother.

"Just let them be, if you don't mind. I'll decide when they want a wash."

"I don't know how you can wear such things, a lovely girl like you," Grainne said, with a feeble attempt at conciliation. "Why must you run around dressed exactly the same as Dermot?"

Nuala's reply could not have been more ill-chosen, even though, unaware of the circumstances, she made it in all innocence. "I can dress like Dermot if I want to, I suppose," she retorted. "Better than dressing exactly the same as Mrs Grieve!"

Before snuggling down with Dermot the evening before, she had glanced from her window at the gathering below to make sure of her mother's whereabouts; and this chanced to happen in the very moment that Grainne and Mrs Grieve first confronted each other. She was immensely tickled at the sight, assuming that bad luck had led them to choose the same model from one of the Larger Ladies' stores; and if Grainne had only held her peace about her own apparel and Dermot's, she would never have taunted her thus. But Grainne leapt to the conclusion that it was the talk of the town, that Nuala, disappearing for hours after supper as usual, had run into some malicious person who passed it on, and that henceforth it would be one more item in her daughter's arsenal. She felt winded, as by a heavy unscrupulous blow in the solar plexus, and quite unequal to further discussion.

"I do wish you could get up now, darling," she pleaded humbly. "Dinner is early today, as I must hurry on and see how your father is."

"I don't want any 'dinner,' as you call it," Nuala replied, still ruffled. "It must be, I'm putting on weight. I noticed my pants were tight on me yesterday evening."

With that she lay back on the pillows again and firmly closed her eyes.

Grainne was halfway down the stairs before the strangeness of her daughter's remark came home to her in all its force. Her pants were tight on her . . . but they were Dermot's pants. Of course they were tight. Nuala was beautifully slim, with narrow hips, but, all said and done, she was a girl. What natural Christian girl could find a boy's pants other than tight? Yet she had spoken as if they were hers. The idea of their deliberately exchanging them as a token of affection, evidently, was wrong; but then again, how could anyone get out of her pants and into someone else's without being aware of the move? And there were the two flaunting insets, one scarlet, one yellow. Were they, perhaps, interchangeable, buttoned on or otherwise fixed, coming off and on like a badge? It all added up to one more mystery and Grainne felt that there was mystery enough in human life as it was.

At the foot of the stairs she was accosted by Geraldine,

who, apart from a dim-witted cleaner, was the only help she had. She was a curious mixture of aggression and torpor, and almost never without a cigarette in her mouth. Grainne disliked this habit extremely but dared not complain. There was a fag end on the creature's lower lip just now, which wagged up and down as she spoke. "Will I put the dinner on the table?"

"Don't bother, thanks," said her mistress coldly. "I don't care for any luncheon today and Miss Nuala is asleep."

"There never was one for sleeping like that Nuala," Geraldine snorted. "'Tis well for her that can do it."

Grainee's method of dealing with the impertinences of her domestic was to ignore them. Having found her hat and gloves, she made for the halldoor, pausing merely to let Geraldine know she expected to be home again in time for tea.

"Afternoon tea, I suppose," the irrepressible Geraldine cackled after her, in what she believed was a London accent.

Grainne pretended not to hear this either. As she drove along the familiar way to St Padraig's, her troubled thoughts went round and round in her head, like a dog chasing its tail. Matters only grew worse when she got there, to hear that on the doctor's orders the Minister was under heavy sedation. As his wife, said Reverend Mother, Mrs Hoolahan might naturally see him if she chose but there was little to be gained by it, as he was barely conscious and making no sense whatever. In reply to Grainne's anxious inquiries, Mother Joseph would only say that he had been a little upset in the morning, and was silent over the outrage committed by Ruarí na Rigg. This piece of well-intentioned reticence set Grainne's imagination madly to work, fancying every kind of horror from delirium tremens to the final overthrow of her husband's reason.

She was halfway home when the possibility struck her of

Brian's condition having to do with the call from Rigg. What could have been the business so urgent as to bring him out to Capri Heights and send him onward, the whole weary way to St Padraig's? Their Departments did not overlap at any point. Was Brian in danger of losing his job, and had Ruairí come to tip him off? Hardly, for there was no love lost between them. Yet the idea was so dreadful that Grainne could not put it from her. She had assumed that Brian would keep his place as long as the party remained in power, not from any great confidence in his ability but because the Department itself was so nebulous, it scarcely mattered who was in charge. But you could depend on nothing and no one in political life.

By the time she turned in the gates of her house, she felt sure that this was the truth of it; and the one consolation remaining to her was, that Ministers drew the full ministerial pension for ever, had they only held office a single week.

SÍX

The coast was clear. As soon as Nuala heard her mother drive away, she bounded out of bed, fresh as paint. First she pulled off her nightgown and posed before the long mirror, anxiously contemplating her outlines, front and side. Her waist was thin, her belly taut, the hollow in either flank as deep as ever. Then she got on the scales and was equally reassured: she had not gained so much as half an ounce. And yet, last night, her jeans had told a different story. Once, as she sat down, there had been a crack as of stitches giving way, and all the time she remained sitting she had felt a coolness behind, caused by an inch or so of bare flesh between her pants and blouse.

Frowning, she picked up these nether garments and scrutinized them closely. Yes, the rear seam had burst a little at the point of greatest stress. She held them up against herself and looked in the glass again; and now she noticed the scarlet crotch and realized what had happened. It was most alarming. Had her mother realized it too, or had she truly thought the trousers needed a wash? In many ways she was fantastically innocent; in fact, Nuala often wondered how she ever had brought herself to produce nine children. At the same time, where her family was concerned, she was uncomfortably observant, shrewd and nobody's fool. She was a deep one, moreover. The fact of her asking no questions, passing no remark, showing no sign of suspicion, behaving indeed in a humble conciliatory manner, in itself meant nothing. She would tuck things away at the back of her mind for heaven only knew how long and then suddenly, when all danger seemed to be past, boil furiously over with them. Slowly Nuala put on the jeans and went downstairs.

Her intention was to ring up Dermot at once, and see what he had to say of this unfortunate complication. There were several telephones in the house and that in the library was the one she used for calls of a private nature: it was no mere extension but a separate number, so that there was no fear of anyone listening in. But as she opened the door she stopped dead, in amazement. The carpet was strewn with litter, as if a company of tinkers had recently encamped there, and for a moment she thought that burglars must have broken in. Then, advancing into the room, she found that the mess was nothing worse than newsprint and saw what had happened. For this one day Grainne had ordered every single Irish paper, had riffled through them hunting the accounts of her party and then just tossed them on the floor. Geraldine had left them undisturbed, as tidying up after others was something she regarded as not her place.

And this was the one, thought Nuala grimly, who scolded her for flinging clothes about in her own bedroom. Typical! She picked the papers up, folded them sternly one by one and put them on the bureau, keeping only the *Inquirer* to glance through before she made her call: if there was anything of Dermot's there, the first thing he would want to know was if she had seen it.

When it came to reading, Nuala had a peculiar habit of which the nuns at Bambino Gesù had never been able to break her. Whether it was a novel, a play, a story, made no difference: she would begin at random, anywhere, in the middle, towards the end, and finish it before turning back to the start. She did the same with gramophone records, and preferred to arrive at cinemas when the film was halfway through. Now, therefore, she plunged into the second column of the *Inquirer*'s front page without so much as a glance at head- or by-line and read on from there. Dermot had done his work so well that she recognized nothing of the bare bones she herself had furnished the day before: they had blossomed out luxuriantly, with wild women, clownish authorities, resolute but misguided police dogs pinning harmless spinsters by the leg, rich Dublin repartee and a crossfire of over-ripe tomatoes and rotten eggs.

Having savoured these descriptive passages to the full, she now went back as her custom was to paragraph one. Like a good reporter, Dermot had led off with a bald statement of such hard facts as he possessed, so that the paragraph in question was extremely short. Nevertheless, she had to read it twice, then look for the writer's name, then read it through once more before the wickedness of it sank in. Her last words to her fiancé yesterday had been, Mind now, never a word of this to a soul! Was this how he interpreted them and how he respected her confidence?

She read feverishly on. Nothing, to be sure, was said of her rôle in the affair, but that mercy was small enough. Her mother knew she had been on the excursion and would certainly wonder why she had made no reference to these scandalous doings. And then there was this wretched business of the pants: and oh! the possibility, the likelihood, of her being charged! She had taken no part in that idiotic demo, had offered no contraband for sale, had broken no law; but to stand in the dock and maintain that the things were for her personal use, unmarried as she was, would be every bit as bad or even worse.

She was normally not in the least afraid of her parents; rather, they were in awe of her. Both in their different ways were timorous and insecure: they rarely stood up to anyone at all, and singlehanded almost never. But while there was little communication between them as a rule, they would now and then combine against a third, two to one, emboldened by each other, with amazing ferocity. It had happened only a week ago and on this very point. Dr Macnamara, an old friend, had been dining at Capri Heights and, in the course of the evening's conversation, without any idea of giving offence, had declared his opinion that birth control would very soon be accepted in Ireland as a matter of private conscience. Had he said this to one or the other alone, there would have been no trouble. It would have been a case of 'Maybe you're right, Mac,' or 'You're the one who would know, Mac,' or even 'And just about time, Mac,' with the speaker's true opinion locked away in his or her breast. But the doctor's coming out with it like that in front of the pair produced a veritable pandemonium, beginning with general denunciations of contemporary morals, moving on to particular ones of the doctor's profession and culminating in personal abuse of the bewildered doctor himself.

"Perhaps you'd rather the old methods of keeping population down?" he was finally goaded to ask. "War, famine, disease . . ."

"Now you're talking like a bloody atheist!" the Minister bawled.

"I am an atheist," the doctor retorted, "as well you know."

The Minister did know it well, and in fact was an atheist too. "You needn't go blurting it out, all the same," he said angrily. "I'll not hear a word against the Faith in this house."

"Bad for business, eh?"

With that the evening broke up in disorder.

Nuala could picture the two of them roaring at her in similar vein, but far more bitterly. She was their child, not a family friend, and she was practising what the doctor merely put forward as a theory. Moreover, in their idiom, she was a lost, a fallen girl. All other sins, envy, avarice, pride, vindictive anger, fraud, might be condoned and even admired in the Island of Saints and Scholars, but not those of the body. Yet what was there her parents could do but roar? She was of age, with a vote. They could hardly beat her or lock her up. If they turned her out of the house she would go and live with Dermot in open sin until they married, and how Dublin would chuckle at that! They would put up with anything rather than expose themselves to ridicule, of that she was certain. But it was her head running on in this way, while her heart remained full of misgiving and apprehension: there was a great deal more of Grainne in her than she knew.

She rang up Dermot and said she must meet him in town at once.

"You saw my hit in the paper?" he asked immediately. Friends, colleagues, even rivals, had patted him on the back all morning and he could think of nothing else.

"We can't talk over the 'phone," Nuala snapped. Despite the automatic system, some ancestral memory of rural eavesdroppers lingered in her mind. "Where'll I find you?"

"Do you want some lunch?"

"No no no."

"In the Green, then, usual place?" He sounded a little aggrieved. "You might say something about my hit."

"I'm going to," Nuala promised, and abruptly rang off.

She strode out to the garage, fastened on her crash helmet and raced off to Dublin on the Yamaha, weaving in and out of the traffic to the accompaniment of furious bursts from motorcar horns. The meeting-place was at the further end of Stephens Green, beside the statue of Lord Ardilaun, halfway between Dermot's flat in the upper reaches of Harcourt Street and the *Inquirer*'s office on the quay: their arrangements were usually made with an eye to his convenience. He was not yet there when she arrived and this was as usual too. He could never bear to be first at their appointments, but was so prompt a second that she often suspected him of hiding somewhere in the vicinity until she had appeared. She had scarcely parked her motorcycle and walked the few paces to the elegant statue, whose lap today was full of empty Guinness bottles, than he rushed up, out of breath and in tearing high spirits, with the *Inquirer* under his arm.

Her reproaches had no effect on him at all. His way with troubles not his own was so light, so calm and easy, that it was time lost merely bringing them up. How had he betrayed her confidence, when she had only told him what was known to scores of others? Who was to know where and how he got his information? Journalists would go to gaol before they revealed their source, and anyhow he wrote the piece as if he had witnessed the demo himself. And again he impressed on her that, were she charged, she need only issue a firm denial. Someone had planted the stuff on her: she was desperate to get home for a party and spoke without thinking: the customs and guards had lost their heads and exceeded their duties: they had no business carting her off to the Bridewell and they'd be lucky men if she didn't sue.

His buoyant tone now changed to one of pathos as he told her of the baby giraffe and the threat its demise had been to himself.

"Would you rather I had the sack?" he asked tragically, putting an arm round her shoulder. "How were we to get married then? As it is, they're all delighted and talking about promotion. Backbiter is off to Fleet Street—suppose they give me that!" 'Backbiter' was Dublin's pet name for the *Inquirer*'s columnist, who signed himself 'Ring-sider' and was reckoned a force. "You worry too much over trifles, Nuala me love! We must take the world as we find it.

"Especially now, with the hard times coming for us all," he went on persuasively, as she still said nothing. "Look here!" He felt in the hip pocket of the pants he was wearing and brought out a little cardboard box, which he opened. "Six reefers," he said, with a flourish as he offered her one, "and guess what they cost me! A third again as much as the lot before. Things are gone skyhigh. Money has lost all value. Twenty pounds melts in a flash. It'll be as much as we can do to keep our heads above water."

Aware that Dermot's supply of red herrings was inexhaustible, Nuala threw in the sponge. "Give me a light, then, thanks," she said listlessly. "And we'd better go somewhere more private."

They strolled as far as the ambiguous tribute to Yeats by Henry Moore and sat on one of the stone benches, pulling the delicious smoke of the herb into their lungs.

"I can take the world all right," Nuala presently said, as she felt herself reviving. "It's the family—that's my problem. Of all the diabolical institutions!"

"That reminds me," Dermot said with a high-pitched giggle. The drug was beginning to send him too. "The poor old *Argus* has come to grief."

Of all the papers in Dublin, or indeed Ireland, the *Globe* led in orthodox piety, printing in full the utterances of any Catholic priest, no matter how familiar to the public. Yesterday it was the Bishop of Killygobragh, bewailing yet again the modern neglect of the evening household rosary: whereas Magee, short of material as he was, had consigned his lordship to the basket without so much as reading him through, the *Globe* had gone to work with a will. BISHOP WARNS NATION! was the headline, and should have been followed by DANGER TO FAMILY LIFE. Through a compositor's slip, however—or as some believed by deliberate sabotage —this came out as DANGER OF FAMILY LIFE. The *Globe* was shattered: the Bishop was fit to be tied; and his chaplain had spent an hour on the phone that morning to dictate the terms, settle the prominence and stipulate the heaviest blackest print for the editor's apology on the morrow.

As usual, the story gained immensely through being told by Dermot. The misprint was a fact, but all else was decoration. By the time his recital was done, Nuala was shaking with laughter: her troubles were fast receding, drifting away like the smoke of the cigarette itself. Parents, bishops, police, summonses, became somehow shadowy and remote, things of no substance. Nothing was real but the warmth of the sun, the flowers, the waterfowl swimming about the lake, Dermot beside her. There was a delicious haziness in her head: she pulled off her helmet, shook out her hair, glanced curiously round as if wondering where exactly she could be. Now something felt hot on her lip. She had come to the end of her smoke and, throwing the stub away, languidly put out a hand for another.

"Wow!" said Dermot. "Having yourself a trip!"

There was a streak of the puritan in this youth, who

prided himself on knowing when to stop and always said: If you trip, don't drink, and if you drink, don't trip. It worried him that Nuala did both, and so freely. If at eighteen and fresh from the convent she already swigged her doubles and trebles, there was no telling what she would do at twenty-five. He did not want her to end up in St Ursula's, the women's counterpart of St Paddy's. As for the reefers, he considered that one at a time was enough. To be hooked was to be tied down, and no one should ever allow himself to be that; and then there was the horrifying expense of it all. But just for once, just for today, flown as he also was, as much with the glory of his front-page article as with the herb, he yielded without a murmur.

"Try and make it last," he advised her, nonetheless. "Look at me, only halfway through. It does more for you, going slow."

Nuala was trying to focus her mind on something she had to say which kept eluding her, swinging up and then away like a. pendulum in tantalizing fashion. Frowning, she leaned forward, elbows on knees, in an effort of concentration, whereupon a crack from behind and a sense of greater comfort put an end to her difficulty.

"I'm wearing your pants," she confided, "and you're wearing mine. It was dressing in all that hurry."

"So that's it!" Dermot exclaimed. "And I thought I was losing weight!"

"And I thought I was putting it on!"

This struck them both as divinely funny.

"I caught Mummy with them," Nuala went on, but it no longer seemed of the slightest importance. "I was in bed, making out to be asleep, and she picked them up and looked at them in a probing sort of way. Felt in the pockets too. Funny, how she can never mind her own business."

"The flash is a different colour," Dermot said. "She must have noticed it. I wonder we didn't."

"And what if she did? When she sees me in my own again, she'll only think she was wrong, if she hasn't forgotten altogether. She's not at all the consecutive type. But we'd best change over now, while we think of it."

"Surely not here?"

"Why not? There's only old Yeats to see us."

"And who'd ever guess which way he was looking?" But Dermot still had a foot on the ground. "We'll go up to the look-out round the corner, will we?" he suggested. "There's shrubs and trees all round it, and we'd see anyone coming before they saw us."

"Okay, then," Nuala sighed. "I just feel this minute like there was no one but you and me in the world!"

The feeling was delightful to her, and so was the sensation she had of floating as together they made their way to the point in question. Dermot had chosen well. Behind them rose a little wooded knoll, screening them from the main walk that ran all round the Green, and in front was only the lake, deserted but for incurious ducks and moorhen, placidly swimming or diving as the fancy took them. The lunch-hour was over and nobody scuttled across the bridge further up: such people as remained were sprawling in deck chairs out of sight round the central flowerbed and taking the sun. Even the park attendants apparently were enjoying a siesta, and the sense gained on Dermot too that if not exactly alone in the world at any rate they had the Green to themselves.

This sense of isolation, however, was purely subjective, induced by the drug; and barely were their garments off than its fallacy was exposed. Somewhere very near at hand a woman was calling her dog, and the sound was coming towards them. "Rusty, Rusty, Rusty! Come on out of it, you little divil!" she commanded. Now they discovered, as many in similar case before them, that while parts of their brain were unusually clear and alive others had more or less ceased to function. Instead of exchanging the pants and briskly putting them on, Dermot fumbled in Nuala's pair for the box of reefers and Nuala let that of Dermot fall to the ground, after which, their practical resource used up, they stood passively waiting until the owner of the voice and dog came into view.

Dublin is a large swollen city, containing roughly a sixth of the country's population. Nevertheless, it is rare indeed to walk about it without running across somebody you know; and that somebody, as may also be worthy of remark, is often the last person alive you would wish to see. And the present was no exception to the rule. The newcomer was Mrs Peggy O'Rourke, flushed and out of breath from her exertions, and too full of her own affairs to notice anything immediately.

"Why, it's Nuala Hoolahan! Have you seen a red setter bitch up here?" she demanded without preamble. "I shall catch it if any of those keepers come along. But I have to let her off the lead, otherwise she won't perform, those highly bred dogs never will. Can't say I blame them. But now she's run off, she's only a pup . . ."

At this point the flow of words suddenly ceased, and Mrs O'Rourke's protruberant eyes travelled from Nuala to Dermot and back to Nuala again.

"Holy Fly!" she ejaculated, after a pause. "Is it training you are, or is this a jumble sale?"

In putting the question, she had no idea whatever of giving offence. Until she married, hockey had been her passion, and now in her widowhood jumble sales played a significant part; so that she merely drew on matters to the fore in her mind. Both Nuala and Dermot were much annoyed, however; they were still in a world of their own, their deeds the concern of none but themselves. They considered that Mrs O'Rourke should have held her tongue, not realizing that this, for her, was impossible.

"No, we didn't see your dog," Nuala replied in her coldest voice, looking away.

"She'd hardly come up here," Dermot added, civil but distant. "Most likely she's swimming in the pond or running about the grass."

Their interrogator was not so easily put off her stroke. "But you don't tell me what you're at," she persisted. "Are you going in for a swim yourselves? I don't believe it's allowed."

"We're settling a bet, if you wish to know," said Dermot, who would probably have retained his gift for improvisation under a general anaesthetic. Nuala yawned, deliberately rude.

"A bet! Queer old bet!" Mrs O'Rourke barked away in amusement until her thoughts took a swift new turn. "Come to that, I've a bet on myself. Isn't it you that's Dermot Wyllie?"

"It is," Dermot replied, with a slight access of warmth.

"And was it you wrote the famous article in the *Inquirer* this morning?" Mrs O'Rourke proceeded, in the tone of one who expects a negative.

Unconscious of the pit about to open at his feet and all but won over, Dermot proudly confirmed that this was the case.

"Then I've lost!" cried Mrs O'Rourke, in stupefaction. "But how can it be? I don't understand this at all." Her face wore the look of some bemused spectator attempting to fathom an ingenious sleight of hand. "I was having lunch with me nephew, Eamon, that's on the *Globe,* and we got to talking about this article, and Eamon said the Dermot Wyllie who wrote it and Nuala's boy friend were one and the same. Now there's where you're wrong, says I. How so? says he—he doesn't like it at all when anyone tells him that. Would you like to bet? says he. I would indeed and a fiver too, says I. Done! says your man: and now show the cards. I'll have to make a 'phone call first, says I, and after that you may count the money out for me. Well, to make a long story short, I rang up Grainne and she wasn't at home. But was I not right, and were you not at the party yesterday? So how could you be there and at Connolly Station at one and the same time?"

Lost in a dream of lunchers all over Ireland discussing the Wyllie sensation, Dermot had been listening with only half an ear. Now he realized that the woman's prattle had ended with some inquiry to which, goggling at him, she awaited an answer.

"Sorry, what was that? I didn't quite catch . . ."

Mrs O'Rourke obligingly ran through the argument again, and Dermot felt his blood turn cold. At the party he had taken pains to keep out of sight, especially the sight of his colleagues, because he was not supposed to be there. He had lurked in the shrubbery until the marquee filled and then sneaked into it, swallowed up in the hordes of thirsty men, few of whom would recognize him or give it a thought if they did. His intention was to remain *perdu* until the betrothal was announced, when he would briefly emerge before hurrying away for good, a man to whom business always came first.

It was a roundabout way of doing things, but Dermot mistrusted ways that were not. To ask the editor for an afternoon off, simple as it might appear to many, raised in his mind all manner of difficulties and complications. Perhaps it would be refused, or the editor would want to know why, or it would be chalked up against him, or he would be expected to make up the time when it was least convenient: no good ever came of showing your hand. And the event had proved him right. There had been no announcement and hence no story to supplement that of the baby giraffe: but this plum of a demo was dropped in his lap as if

72

by Providence, and he had redeemed himself ten times over.

He could have sworn that only Grainne knew for a fact who he was and that he was there. He had never met the Julia Someone she was with, and she had not introduced them. After a quick disparaging glance at his jeans on arrival, she had made no attempt to bring him forward and seemed, if anything, pleased at his lying low. Nuala was as little anxious for recognition as he and they had made their way into the house circuitously, hidden by bushes. And yet this old hairo with the Pekinese eyes had spotted him and was betting on it against—of all people—Eamon Kelly of the *Globe*!

"I'm afraid Eamon wins," he told her, with a sympathetic shake of his head.

"But I saw you meself!" cried Mrs O'Rourke. "I peeped into the tent, looking for Justice McCann, and saw you large as life, swallowing 7-up."

"That settles it, then," Dermot declared. "It'll have been my brother. I never take 7-up."

"Brother? what brother? are you not Professor Wyllie's boy?" asked Mrs O'Rourke, growing ever more bewildered. "Hasn't he five daughters and only one son, and isn't that all the trouble?"

"How d'you mean, trouble?" Dr Wyllie's heir demanded, irate.

"Nuala . . ."

Still not looking at their tormentor, Nuala crammed her helmet on and adjusted the straps without a word.

"Leave Nuala out of it, do you mind? She isn't over the unpleasantness in the North."

"But . . ."

They might have continued like this indefinitely, Mrs O'Rourke putting one foot in it after the other and Dermot sinking deeper and deeper into a swamp of fiction. At this moment, however, Rusty came bounding up with an air, common to truant dogs, of having searched for her mistress high and low. An animal of strong emotions but limited powers of expression, she first sent Mrs O'Rourke reeling with a few ecstatic kisses. Then she seized the box of reefers from Dermot, chawed it up, prepared to swallow it, hesitated, changed her mind and spat the fragments out. Smiling broadly and waving her feathery tail, she looked round for some new outlet to her limitless *joie de vivre*. Dermot's pants lay on the ground as if placed there for no other purpose, and she immediately galloped off with them, down the path and along the side of the lake, pausing now and then to toss the garment in the air and catch it again before she galloped on.

"God help us, I'll never get her now," lamented the owner, all else forgotten, as she lumbered away in pursuit.

The lovers were down to earth again, the smokes having died in them as drink dies in the airborne at a suspicion of engine trouble.

"What'll we do now?" asked Nuala plaintively.

"My pants! Our reefers! That bloody bitch! And the woman's another, poking and prying and making bets! She'll ring your mother up and then I've had it."

"She'll maybe forget."

"With five pounds in it? Not she." He meditated glumly awhile, and then burst out, "For the love of God, will you put those pants on? Are you sound enough to ride home, or will you go in a taxi?"

Sullenly clothing herself, Nuala said she was sound as a bell, why wouldn't she be? She was tempted to ask who had got them into this pickle, but was wise enough to refrain. All her forebodings crowded back as, after taking a perfunctory leave, she returned to the Yamaha and set off for home. As for Dermot, he had no option but to sprint to his flat, as if indeed he were in training, like some bloody athlete from U.C.D. It was utterly ridiculous that, head up, elbows in, knees lifting, he could lope along in his briefs unmolested, whereas if he merely walked he might be stopped by a Guard.

His surmise concerning Mrs O'Rourke was correct. Exhausted as she was by the recovery of her bitch, which took the better part of an hour, she was on to Eamon Kelly within minutes of reaching her house. To him she told all, not omitting the detail of Dermot's phantom brother, and was much surprised at the jubilation caused by her news.

"But you owe me five pounds, remember?" she insisted, thinking this point had somehow been overlooked.

"So I do, so I do," replied Kelly without hesitation and, chortling, put the receiver down.

seven

In his account of the *Globe* and the Bishop of Killygobragh, Dermot had drawn freely on his powers of inven-
tion, as has been said. The *Inquirer* newsroom was chuckling over the misprint as he came in that morning, but
left off at once to shower congratulations on him for yesterday's scoop. Shortly afterwards, there was a bomb scare in
the Revenue Commissioner's office at the Castle: a sinister-
looking package had been found in a filing cabinet, and
the military and the Guards were already on their way.
Dermot was chosen to cover the incident and, with a vision
of still more headlines, departed with alacrity. When he
got to the Castle, everything was held up by the de-fusing

expert, whom no one had been able to contact so far; and when at last he appeared and opened the parcel, which proved to contain somebody's lunch, the morning was nearly gone. Dermot notified the office and, this being his afternoon off, went straight home, where he was just in time to receive Nuala's call. Accordingly, he missed the gossip at the reporters' midday assembly in Mooney's, of which the Bishop and the *Globe* were the main topic.

It is difficult, with the best will in the world, to invent anything much about the Irish. Those foolish enough to attempt it fling up their hands in despair, seeing their wildest notions left at the post by reality. The Bishop of Killygobragh had done everything so gaily imputed to him by Dermot, and more besides. He wanted damages for himself and punishment of the guilty, as well as the grovelling retraction. He was carrying on, as his brethren had successfully carried on, thirty or forty years ago. The winds of change howling across the world from Rome had not ruffled a hair of his head. The papal hint that, on reaching a certain age, bishops should consider retirement, had left him unmoved. A bishop was as old as he felt, he was wont to declare, and no one ventured to ask how old, in his case, that might be.

The *Globe,* for whom no Churchman was ever wrong, would have found its position unhappy at any time; but in days gone by it would have humbled itself and complied with his Lordship's every demand. Now, however, it found itself in a cleft stick. New and redoubtable forces were emerging, not least of which, from an editor's point of view, was the Printers' Union. At this very moment there were rumblings and grumblings galore, threats of go-slow if not of strike. The men were dissatisfied with their pay, their conditions, their status, and, above all, the slightest breath of criticism was anathema to them. They could, and did, misspell names, print words back to front, transpose or repeat whole lines, turn them upside down or leave them out altogether; and if the matter were brought to their notice they flew into a rage. To comment on such a trifle as printing 'of' for 'to,' let alone discipline the operator responsible, was bound to lead to a walkout.

Mr Fergus O'Grady, the editor, wished with all his heart that the Republic were the priest-ridden slave state of Ulster Protestant belief. He billed and coo'd to the Episcopal chaplain on the telephone while desperately trying to avoid a firm commitment. He must have time, he said: a matter as grave as this must go to the Board. And the Board were all on their holidays except for the Chairman, who was in the Top Security wing of St Paddy's. The chaplain was insistent, however, and might well have carried the day if, providentially, the line to Killygobragh had not broken down in the middle of the talks and put an end to communication for twenty-four hours. But it would be resumed: O'Grady had no illusions on that point, and set about his daily work conscious of the sword hanging over his head.

"We'll boost the Rosary tomorrow," he said to his deputy, Eamon. " 'Every time you recite a Hail Mary, a tremor runs through Hell'—that class of thing. Fr Nagle can do it."

"Fr Nagle prefers to choose a theme for himself."

"So he does. Fr Clancy, then. And I'll beat the living daylights out of the *Inquirer,* over that women's demo."

It was always a comfort to Mr O'Grady, in his hours of darkness, to lash out at somebody else.

"I was going to speak to you about that business," said Eamon Kelly. This conversation was taking place at the end of the morning, before he went to lunch with his aunt. "There's something odd about it. I made inquiries here and there, and there's no confirmation. Wyllie mentioned women being carted off to the Bridewell—our man there wasn't on duty, but he tells me there are no women in custody now and no record of any arrests. Same with the Customs. First thing anyone heard of it."

"Only means that somebody wants it hushed up."

"But how can you hush it up, when it's all over town?"

"Eamon, I'm surprised at you," said his editor wearily. "They'll say it's all a pack of lies and dare the *Inquirer* to prove them wrong.

"And that's what I'll say too!" he exclaimed, with kindling eye as the thought took hold. "I was going to say that public decency demanded such things be ignored. But from what you tell me, I'm safe to go ahead with a gross slander on Irish womanhood. If that and the Rosary together don't sweeten his Lordship, I'll eat his biretta!"

He was engrossed in this work of edification when, at about half-past four, Eamon burst into the room, evidently bringing news of importance.

"Hold on there a minute," the editor said, annoyed at the interruption and typing away like mad. '. . . in our opinion the whole affair of this now notorious article is as baffling as unsavoury. There is a Fleet Street axiom, dog does not eat dog, and therefore we mention no names. But on behalf of the maligned women of Ireland we do press for a full and public inquiry. Our people surely have a right to know how these extraordinary allegations ever came to be made.'

"Well, what is it?" he inquired testily, having by no means done.

"Just this, Wyllie was never at the station when the Belfast train arrived. He was at Grainne Hoolahan's party, out Dalkey way. I got that from my aunt, who was there as well. I happened to say that the Wyllie who wrote the article was the lad that's going about with Nuala Hoolahan, and she said it couldn't be. We had a bet on it, though it seemed like only taking her money. And just now she rang up to say she was right. She had come across Wyllie this afternoon in Stephens Green and faced him with it, and he told her, pleased as Punch, he wrote the article all right but that it was his brother she saw. He hasn't got a brother! And he was in a secluded spot of the Green with Nuala Hoolahan, and both of them had their pants off. Now!"

The editor's brain fairly reeled under this torrent of information. "Leave their pants out of it, we'll attend to those later," he said joyously. "About this party—what kind of a party was it?"

"An afternoon garden party. We sent a camera man. The picture is on page seven."

"To be sure, so it is," said the editor hastily, unwilling to admit that the Bishop's headline was as far as he had read. "And he never told you of Wyllie's being present?"

"He wouldn't have seen him, he took his shots outside in the sun. It seems Wyllie was lying low in the refreshment marquee. My aunt only saw him because she looked in there, thinking to find someone she knew. But every pressman got a list of the people invited—trust Mrs Hoolahan! —and Wyllie's name was on it."

"That still wouldn't prove he was there." But the editor was merely playing the *advocatus diaboli*: he was fully convinced and now leaned back in his chair as if overcome. "The nerve! the gall!" he cried. "Dozens of others besides your aunt will have seen him."

"They mightn't have known who he was."

The editor smiled at the very notion of that. "Everyone in Dublin knows who everyone is," he observed.

"Well, they wouldn't be thinking about him in the marquee, once their noses were down in the bucket."

Mr O'Grady picked up Dermot's article, on the desk beside him for handy reference. "Will you listen to this?" he appealed. " 'I never saw hand-to-hand fighting to match it for sheer ferocity, and as for the screeching, my ears are a-tingle with it yet. You'd have said a thousand peacocks were hollering for their corn.' "

"I know."

"Well! Bravo, Eamon. We'll send your auntie a bunch of roses. And now let me get to work."

He read his editorial through, struck out the last five lines and recast them as follows:

'We are forced to the view that the whole affair of this now notorious article is not just unsavoury but baffling as well. The absence of all confirmation, referred to above, is not the only or even the most bewildering feature in the case. What we are offered here is a vivid firsthand account of happenings at Connolly station; and yet we in this office know for a fact that the man who wrote it was miles and miles away at the time they are alleged to have taken place. Far be it from us, of all men, to deny the miraculous or the supernatural; but we are bound to confess that the idea of a reporter in two places at once is one we have difficulty in accepting. There is a good old Fleet Street axiom to the effect that dog does not eat dog, and therefore we mention no names. But on behalf of the maligned women of Ireland, we do press for a full and public inquiry. Our people surely have a right to know the truth of this most singular, indeed inexplicable, proceeding.'

He sent the finished product down to the printer immediately, ordering the proof to be brought to him, as too precious for any mere sub to handle. It struck him as even better in print than in typescript and he read it over and over, enjoying it more every time. The printer had inadvertently set up the phrase 'full and public inquiry' as 'full and pubic inquiry' but he was too elated to notice this and marked the galley OK with a flourish. Then he went happily home, his mind full of thoughts and dreams for the morrow, the claims of the bishop forgotten.

Mrs O'Rourke telephoned twice during the evening, with further news of some description and also to inquire when she was to expect her money. She did not get past Eamon's secretary, who knew the voice well, but Eamon was informed and, after the first call, left word that he would look in on the way to his office tomorrow. The news apparently concerned his aunt's dog and, busy in the editor's absence, Eamon assumed it was just her usual chatter; and when he got to her house in the morning and she started pouring it into his ears, he listened with resignation.

Rusty had capered about for a while, enjoying herself with the stolen pants until she saw her mistress toiling along in her wake. Then she dropped them and stood wagging her tail, as if begging they might be thrown for her again. Mrs O'Rourke picked them up, tucked them under her arm and grimly produced the lead: whereupon Rusty was off in a flash, shooting over the ground with the speed of an electric hare. Only after a long chase and with the help of many bystanders was she recaptured and brought home to Ailesbury Road in the car. It was now that Mrs O'Rourke realized the bitch was not herself. Going into the house, she staggered repeatedly as if drunk, and crawled into her basket. Thinking she was worn out, Mrs O'Rourke left her to rest while she telephoned to Eamon to claim her winnings; but when this was done, she came for another look and found the bitch in a heavy sleep from which she could not be roused.

Alarmed, she rang up the vet and gave him a full account of the case, so full that the busy man suggested she bring the animal in. Rusty was carried, unconscious, into the clinic and laid upon the couch. The vet examined her carefully, listened to her heart, smelled her breath and looked puzzled.

"She couldn't have got hold of some amphetamine pills,

or anything like that, I suppose?" he asked. "It seems to me, she is drugged."

Mrs O'Rourke repudiated the idea with vehemence.

"Then I'll take a saliva test, if you don't mind waiting," said the vet. "Not to worry, whatever it is, she'll sleep it off."

By this time Eamon was on the borders of sleep himself; but the next part of this seemingly endless and pointless narrative brought him back post-haste.

"And when Mr Purcell had finished he told me," said his aunt with thrilling emphasis, "there was cannabis in the saliva! And he looked at me pretty strangely. I all but dropped dead. My little Rusty! My own little girl! But then I remembered. Dermot Wyllie was holding a small cardboard box and she snatched it from him and chewed it up and spat out the bits again. But it must be there the cannabis was, and she had some of it swallowed in spite of herself!"

"The Lord preserve us!" broke from Eamon's lips. It was not becoming in a deputy editor to show surprise, but the words were out before he could stop them. Pulling himself together, he asked: "Have you the pants there yet?"

"I have!" and she ran to get them.

Eamon went through the pockets and came on the few little items that Grainne had seen and replaced there. "Our old friend Abdul Hamid," he commented. "If it doesn't beat all! Wyllie had best mind himself—they're cracking down on this."

In fact the authorities were inclined to think that fines no longer met the case: one of the last statements from Justice Magadoo, before he entered St Paddy's, was that in future conviction would lead to prison.

"I must be going," Eamon continued. "And I'll take the

pants along. Not a word to a soul, Aunt Peggy, even if
you bust. I'm serious."

"And the money!" cried Mrs O'Rourke, as he moved towards the door. "Where's me lovely fiver?"

Eamon handed over the lovely fiver and went his way,
very much pleased with the world.

eight

Now the long comatose holiday period really began. As when a motion picture is stopped, with all on the screen frozen in their tracks, everything came to a halt until those who were away returned to set it moving again.

Even the Bishop of Killygobragh was fobbed off by the absence of the *Globe* chairman and directors. The editor published an apology for the misprint but insisted that damages and retribution were not matters for him; and with this his Lordship had to be content although, as he observed to his chaplain, if the paper thought he would ever let go they little knew their man.

More serious was the affair of the *Globe* attack on the *In-*

quirer. Dermot had no difficulty in convincing Magee that their charges were wholly unfounded. It was true, he said, that he had looked in for a moment at Capri Heights. While at Connolly he had spotted Nuala Hoolahan among the crowd and having taken his notes of the fracas there and followed up with inquiries at the Bridewell, he had dashed off to her house to see if there were anything she could add. In support of this, he produced a note of taxi fares, amounting to several pounds.

Greatly incensed by the aspersion on the paper's integrity, already put out by the official silence over the incident, Magee instructed his solicitors. O'Grady's article, which had given him such pleasure to write, was no mere damp squib, therefore, but a boomerang: a boomerang, however, poised motionless in the air until such time as Mr Florence Chase, of Chase & Garner, should wend his homeward way from St Tropez. Unaware of this, O'Grady took Magee's silence as an admission of guilt and kept up a flow of jeers and innuendoes, all of which went on the file.

Eamon Kelly too was forced to bide his time until a friend of his, a forensic analyst, should be available to examine the pockets of Dermot's jeans, locked away in a fireproof safe.

Even the bowsie man who had so often plagued the country's leaders appeared to be on vacation. At least nothing was seen or heard of him since he had been found asleep in the National Library and escorted out. Once he was gone, as usual, people talked about him and claimed to know who he was, from where and of what his grievance consisted. All their claims were different and all were wrong.

As the days went by and the Gardai left her in peace, Nuala concluded that the matter of her alleged offence was closed and all but forgot it herself. Dermot went with his mother to Spain and she was free to pine for him to her heart's content. Constantly, when they were together, something would happen that threw a shadow: the other day, for instance, his airy unconcern for her worries and the heavy weather he made of his own had troubled her deeply. Grainne had warned her what to expect, saying that all men were selfish and this one a mother's darling to boot; and riding home on the Yamaha she had felt as if she were married already. But now he was gone, a thousand miles away in Marbella, and she dreamed of him, of his handsome face, the sound of his voice, his touch, from morning to night.

For Grainne also things were going well. The authorities at St Padraig's had strongly urged that Brian remain there for some weeks, in the hope of a lasting cure. Nothing stirred on the political front, they said, and the opportunity was too good to miss: it was frustrating for themselves, this regular drying-out of a man only to see him back in a month or so. Happy among his friends, Brian was willing and Grainne even more so; and accordingly it was settled.

There was a double satisfaction in this, because with Brian away she could hope for visits from the rest of the family. They would not come while he was there, not even the eldest, Liam, who if anything drank more than Brian did but was as prudish about his father as if he never swallowed a drop. The six surviving children of the marriage formed, as it were, a pageant of the Hoolahan fortunes. There was Liam, Brian's spit and image, who carried on the auctioneering business down in the country, much expanded these days by the political connection. Next was a daughter, Julia, known as Joola until she was twelve, when Grainne discovered the way to pronounce it, and now in religion as Sister Dolours. After her came a second son, Matt, who likewise had the vocation and was a Catholic Curate in Kerry. To have given two of their offspring to the Church was a source of pride to the parents, as well as a guarantee of their standing; but enough was enough. Brian was prospering and turning his mind to politics when the next boy was born: they named him for Edward FitzGerald and sent him to Clongowes and University College. He was now an attorney in Mullingar. Caitlin, who followed him, was educated by the Ursulines and 'abroad' —which meant six months in a convent near Brussels—and had married a director of Irish Airlines.

These births came at intervals of a year, the only gaps being caused by the three demises; and after that Grainne had a respite of six years, until Nuala turned up unexpectedly.

Now Grainne had hopes of seeing them all and it was merely a question of fitting them in. If Liam were there, none of the rest would come, nor could Sister Dolours and Fr Matt be asked together. In their childhood she had bossed and even bullied him in the older-sister's way and when, with his ordination, he took precedence of her in the family and authority over herself, she never adapted to a state of affairs so unnatural. She could not see him without yielding to envious and uncharitable thoughts, and so avoided him as an occasion of sin. Both of them got along pleasantly with Edward FitzGerald and Caitlin, however, and these two were actually fond of each other: the difficulties were not insurmountable. It was finally arranged that Liam should come first, on his own, then Fr Matt with Edward FitzGerald, wife and children, then Sister Dolours with Caitlin, husband and baby twins.

Liam was not married, or likely to be. He had been engaged for upwards of nine years to a local woman, the sister of a rival auctioneer; but whenever she hinted at the desirability of their fixing a day he would hurriedly speak of something else. With business flourishing after Brian's entry into politics, there was no longer a valid reason for the match and nobody in Duncommon would have criticized Liam for simply calling it off. He declared, however, that this was the lady's privilege and, until such time as she availed herself of it, continued to see her once or twice a month.

Grainne doted on her eldest child, waited on him hand and foot and turned a blind eye to all manner of doings which, had Brian been guilty of them, would have led to a scene. She could hardly wait for him to arrive and crossed the days off the calendar, like a small girl expecting a treat. "I shall ask Dr Macnamara in while Li-Li is here," she announced to Nuala. "Most people get on his nerves, but he is always glad to see old Mac."

"And what makes you think old Mac will come, after the pasting he got last time?" Nuala inquired.

"Ah, stop your nonsense, it was all good fun."

"I always thought he had a sense of humour!" she complained, after ringing the doctor up. Not only had he refused, but he gave no reason why and expressed no polite regret. "It must be, he's offended. You'd have cut yourself on the edge of his voice."

"And that surprises you?"

"It certainly does. He should be glad, getting asked to a decent house again, after what he said." Grainne was working herself up. "We had to let him know what we thought, but it could have all been forgotten next day."

The hurling of insults at night, followed by amnesty in the morning, was very much a part of their social pattern.

"He said nothing but what lots of people say," Nuala objected.

"They'd as well not say it in front of me, then."

"That a change is coming? But it's come. Even the law is different." She was wasting her breath. It was like arguing with a block of stone.

"Is it the law? That's only for the people in the North, so

that Ireland can be united. It's the Holy Father will tell us what to do, not the law. Nuala!" There was a sudden fear in Grainne's eyes. "Don't tell me you are falling away? getting wicked modern ideas? As true as you stand there, I would rather see you dead."

"Ah, leave me out of it," was all the reply that came, in a weary mutter.

"Yes, and you might have been left out of it too, if your father and I had done as you seem to think we should."

With that she swept from the room, to make sure of the last word. There was no need for her to do this, as for once she really had scored a bull's-eye. To Nuala, the thought of a world that did not contain herself was so novel and startling as to take her breath away.

There was, then, no company for Liam during the ten days of his visit, except what he found for himself in the Dalkey public houses. He had nothing against this state of affairs, in fact it suited him down to the ground. He had his own routine, and followed it as strictly as any athlete in training. At ten o'clock Grainne brought up an ample breakfast cooked by herself, and he picked it over and drank half a cup of tea. By eleven he was downstairs, looking for a 'cure' of export ale, and at a quarter past he left for the Smuggler's Cave or the Witches' Chair or Rooney's. At three he reappeared with a bottle under his arm and spent a couple of hours with his mother, chatting and drinking and biting vaguely into the sandwiches she had cut. On the stroke of five he was off, not to be seen again until the houses shut, often brought home in a strange car by an unknown man and needing help upstairs to bed. Whenever this happened, Grainne would walk to town first thing in the morning, trace his car and bring it back, ready for use as required. Far from resenting this schedule, Grainne admired it and would proudly remark that, apart from herself, Liam was the only one in the family with any sense of time.

Everything passed off as usual except that, on Liam's last day, in the course of their afternoon chat he brought the conversation round to his father. No reference was made to the Minister's habits, but his present location was causing Liam concern.

"You'll agree, Mammy, it doesn't look too good?" he inquired, topping up a dark brown tumblerful of whisky and water as he spoke. "Why couldn't he stay at home, like anyone else?"

"He's only in for the rest, while the others are all away," Grainne pleaded. "And a lot of his friends are with him. Fellows he doesn't get time to see when the Dáil is sitting."

"I still say, he should think more of us and less of himself. There's a good deal of local talk." But Liam left it at that and, as he applied himself to the whisky, his thoughts soon wandered away.

The other members of the family were more interested in Nuala's engagement than in their father's doings, which they had long accepted as part of life. The two religious were strongly averse to the match. Fr Matt had been appalled by Dermot's article which, he declared, should never have been written or printed, don't mind if it were the truth or not. It betrayed a subversive spirit that made him unsuitable as the head of an Irish family, and Nuala was far too young to lead him in better ways. Journalists too— Fr Matt had never come across one—were all feckless, bohemian, unprincipled and given to emigration. For her part, Sister Dolours raised evey possible argument against it, but this she was wont to do when any marriage was contemplated. She was also deeply shocked by what she termed the 'modernistic' way it had come about, in that Nuala, a chit of a girl, should have accepted the boy and coolly announced the fact instead of first consulting her elders. Marriage, if marriage there must be, was the affair of the family, not of the individual. Dermot should have been arraigned before them all, the pros and cons of the matter thoroughly discussed, and a consensus of opinion taken, as had been done in the case of Liam, Edward FitzGerald and Caitlin.

Edward FitzGerald agreed with all that Fr Matt had to say, while Caitlin heartily seconded the views of Sister Dolours. Thus the family talks went on in a spirit of harmony, with the priest and the nun repeating themselves over and over again and the brother and sister giving a cordial assent. The private ideas of both, to be sure, ran on entirely different lines. Edward FitzGerald, the attorney, was greatly tickled by the rumours of legal action that reached his ears and thought the whole affair was excellent fun. Caitlin was quick to see that a journalist in the family might be useful in the promotion of Irish Airlines. They took their mother aside and calmed her fears with these opinions which, however, they gave in strictest confidence. And so it went on, with people saying one thing and thinking another in decent Irish style, and the visits went off without a single jarring note to spoil the general pleasure. Grainne felt almost young again, what with Edward's children running about the house and getting over-excited, and then after that, Caitlin's babies squalling and being sick; and added to this, when Nuala put in a rare appearance, she was on unusually good behaviour. All in all, it was the happiest summer Grainne had known in a long time, and when at last it drew to a close she faced the future with an optimism as high as it was wholly without foundation.

nine

The leaves were beginning to change colour when Brian, not without a pang, quitted the friendly walls of St Padraig's. He was looking extremely well, with clear eyes and complexion, and he had lost a stone and a half. Sister Lourdes sang his praises as she saw him off, calling him her star patient and a credit to the establishment.

"But no celebrations, d'you hear me?" she said. "What we have to avoid, is over-confidence."

Brian promised faithfully to heed her advice.

The only other discharge that morning was Kevin Magadoo, the District Justice. There had been some little doubt in his case, the Senior Consultant inclining to think that it might be premature; but the Justice pleaded so eloquently, pointing out that his long absence from duty might prejudice his career, that in the end the authorities gave way. He and Brian left together, separating awhile in town to busy themselves with haircuts and other small personal errands and meeting again for lunch at their Club. Here they fell in with a nautical friend, and spent a blameless afternoon with him, sailing to Howth and back.

By the time that Brian reached home, he was the very picture of health, and altogether a different man from the one who had entered St Padraig's three months ago. Grainne had naturally been a constant visitor there, but even she was bowled over by his appearance as he stood before her in the hall, brown and fit, with his clothes hanging loosely on him.

"You're looking great, younger than Liam," she cried. "You'll have to go to the tailor tomorrow and get everything taken in."

"Ah, go 'way with you," he answered goodhumouredly. "Is it hunting me out already?"

There was a special welcome-home supper that night, composed of Brian's favourite dishes: lentil soup, pigs' trotters in parsley sauce with fried potatoes and boiled onions, and marmalade pudding. He refused an offer of Coca-Cola to wash it down, and declared that from this day forth he would stick to tea. Strong black tea with plenty of sugar was all he wanted, he said; and a pot of this was quickly prepared and set before him.

He was ravenous after the long hours at sea, and helped himself to everything more than once. For a time the sounds of chewing and swallowing were all that were heard, but then he suddenly asked, "Where's Nu?"

Grainne said their daughter was out for the evening.

"You'd think she'd be here for my first day back," Brian grumbled.

"She was, too, earlier on. We expected you home to din-lunch," Grainne replied. Sister Lourdes had rung up with the news of her patient's departure and a lot of advice about tranquillisers and vitamin pills. "She stayed in till six, then said she must go. Anyhow, she wouldn't touch a meal like this, she's on about her weight again. I'll tell you who is coming in afterwards, though," she went on quick-ly, for Brian's face had clouded. "Old Mac."

And a nice job she'd had of it to persuade him! assuring him that Brian had meant no harm on the last occasion, that he had been overworked and tired, was now complete-ly well and longing to see his old friend. Brian was no more enthusiastic than the doctor himself had been.

"Mac's not me daughter, that I know," he said, frown-ing. "And I couldn't have got here sooner. I had to look in at the office after all this while and sure enough, there was a great heap of stuff there waiting on me."

"Well, when you didn't ring up . . ."

"Ring up? and why should I?" Such a thing had never crossed his mind: he always came and went to suit himself. "You could have guessed where I'd have to go." Oh, the women, the women. No sense in their heads at all.

Thunder was in the air already. Grainne reminded her-self of what Sister Lourdes had said about the need for pa-tience in this awkward time of readjustment. Matters would surely improve, she thought, once the doctor was there and the two friends talking the old days over togeth-er. But Dr Macnamara had barely arrived before they took a turn for the worse.

After what had happened, it was certainly good of him to come at all; but Grainne did feel he might have changed his clothes in honour of so happy an event. And the event was solemn as well as happy, given the impor-tance of the man involved. But there was Mac in the old grey suit, baggy at the knees and with a darn on the elbow, in which he was always attired. The reason for this was merely that it had not occurred to him to do otherwise, but Grainne could never believe that anything was as simple as that. It must be a deliberate snub, or a hint of continuing displeasure, or a display of indifference, even contempt; and she felt both hurt and angry.

Brian read nothing of this into the situation, as he never noticed what anyone wore. It was the way the doctor spoke that jarred on him. At St Padraig's, everything possible was done to spare the inmates' feelings. They were there as sick men, to be nursed back to health like any others, struck down as it might be by 'flu or lumbago or similar afflictions. The cause of their trouble, the fact of it being self-induced, was never referred to except insofar as diagnosis or treatment made this necessary, and then with masterly circumlocution. But Macnamara approached the whole affair in a spirit of levity, cracking jokes in the worst of taste and inquiring into all manner of things that were no concern of his.

"How many times is this, you were in? I left off counting," he said with a chuckle. "It must be, you're qualified for the Old Boys' Tie, or haven't they one?"

"They have not," said Brian, gritting his teeth.

The doctor was no more conscious of Brian's annoyance than Brian had been of the doctor's suit. "They should, then," he continued blithely. "Of a warm mulberry tone, to suit the complexion, and Patsy himself in gold, on horseback, spearing a bottle."

"I'll bring in the coffee," Grainne hastily said.

When she came back with the tray, Brian was shouting, "There's forty million alcoholics in Great Britain, today, so now!"

"Steady on with that," said the doctor. "That's two-thirds of the population."

"And what if it is? It's what I read in one of those surveys."

"Then they'll mostly be from over here, it wouldn't surprise me," smiled the doctor. "And you, wanting to bring them all back!"

"Leave me out of it, will you? And I'll listen to no denigration of the Irish people."

"Isn't it time for your pills?" Grainne put in. "Sister Lourdes said two about now, to start calming you down ready for bed."

Brian fumbled angrily for the bottle of pills, while Dr Macnamara watched him with an amused and tolerant air.

He was enjoying himself, pleased after all to be in the house again, sitting in his usual chair, the old bachelor friend that married people often acquire, so much at home he was almost one of the family. Brian was in an awkward mood, but this was only natural and would soon ease off as the tranquillisers got to work. But his pleasure was short-lived: for something then occurred that was so outrageous, he afterwards declared he would never have thought it possible.

The coffee being finished, Grainne removed the cups. Dr Macnamara waited with pleasant anticipation for the sound of little wheels as she returned, as always, pushing a trolley loaded with glasses and drink. Nothing of the kind, this evening, took place. She came back empty-handed and resumed her seat, merely inquiring if the doctor would prefer his pipe or a cigar.

The significance of the procedure did not at once strike home. Innocently, the doctor replied that, if it were all the same to her, he would try a drop of Scotch. He expected her to leap up in contrition, all apologies for the oversight: instead, she made a humorous little grimace in Brian's direction and murmured, "Ah, Mac, we're on the waggon now."

Her indignant guest could hardly believe his ears. So this was the thanks he got, for his magnanimity in coming here: a dry party with a fretful alcoholic! And what the devil did Grainne mean by 'we'? *He* had not been in St Paddy's. Grainne never drank much and if she chose to abstain altogether for Brian's sake, that was her business. But why rope him in as well? By Dublin standards the doctor was an abstemious man, but a whole evening without Scotch was something he never thought to experience.

It was really too bad. He had agreed to come, he told himself, to get Grainne off the telephone, as she seemed likely to go on arguing and imploring for ever. His intention was to make the evening short, a mere look-in to oblige her, and then away. This was impossible now, for it would look as if he had only come for the Scotch. He must sit out the full two hours or more, unless Brian fell asleep or burst into one of his rages. That might well come to pass, if he brought the conversation round to birth control or some other inflammatory topic, and for a moment he was tempted. But then he rose above it and, deciding to make the best of things, resumed his playful banter as if nothing had put him out.

"Who else got off, apart from yourself?" he began. "And was there a prize-giving first?"

Brian scowled and made no reply.

"Ah, let's leave all that," Grainne said.

"I'm only taking a friendly interest," the doctor protested. "Nothing to be ashamed of, is there?"

"Did you go on your holidays yet?" asked Grainne, a little abruptly.

"Who, me? I don't go on holidays, as you should know by now." This was true and Grainne spoke without thinking. Dr Macnamara always said, it was holiday enough that his patients went away.

"Ah, your ship'll come in yet," said Brian, with a swift back-hander.

The doctor's brows drew balefully together. "I'm not sure I know what you mean," he said.

Tension was building up, with all of them annoyed over something. If this continued, Grainne saw, Brian and she would presently slip into their wonted combination against any defenceless outsider, and one more evening would end in ruins. To prevent this she excused herself, saying there were one or two things in the house to be seen to. As she went through the hall, her eye fell on the suit-case that Brian had brought, and the sight of it cheered her immensely. His habit of leaving it behind at the Home, in readiness for the next visit, had always seemed a reproach to herself. She would take it upstairs, unpack his things and put them away, then bring the case to the attic, hoping it would remain there undisturbed. After that she would return to the men, by which time with luck harmony would be restored.

For a case that should have contained no more than py-jamas, dressing-gown, slippers, brushes and sponge-bag, it was curiously heavy; and when she put it down on the bed an ominous clink from inside made her blood run cold. Hastily, with hands that shook, she undid the fastenings, to find four bottles of whisky lolling about on the clothes. For a moment she was almost ready to faint; but then she saw that, instead of the boldly striped pyjamas that Brian fa-voured, these were of pale lavender with black frogging. The slippers too were of crimson suede, not the tartan felt to which Brian was addicted, and the dressing-gown was of silk to match, rather than grey flannel. And there was even a book there as well, the last thing to be found in Brian's possession. Grainne picked it up and eagerly opened it: on the fly-leaf, written in a tremulous hand, were the words, Property of Kevin Magadoo, District Justice, Dublin.

The relief of it quite took her breath away, making her gasp like a fish on land. And with the relief was remorse at having mistrusted Brian. It was a natural mistake, for the suitcases were identical, black, impersonal, chromium-fitted, such as are seen by the dozen rolling along the belt at airports. But Sister Lourdes had rubbed well into her the need for showing confidence in Brian's recovery, emphasizing that in order to do this she must really have it. All day long she had schooled herself to feel as she ought; and then, at the mere sight of those bottles, her faith had burst like a bubble!

There were sounds of a motor on the drive, and she went to the window. It was the Gardai squad car, informed no doubt of the Minister's return and coming to assure him that surveillance would now be resumed. In troubled times like the present, they kept an eye on everyone of importance, driving continually round and round, sometimes looking in at the house, sometimes posting a Garda at the gate. She had missed them while Brian was away, the solemn young men in the smart uniforms, and their prompt reappearance now was like an augury of settled days to come.

Her mind wholly at peace again, she was watching the car draw near when the telephone rang. It had been switched through to the bedroom during the holidays, as the children were inclined to treat it as a toy, ringing up strangers and hurling jokes or insults at them, and Grainne yet had not switched it back. She took up the receiver, expecting a friendly congratulation or welcoming message for Brian; but instead there was a voice she did not know, sharp, sour, querulous, the very way it asked who was there somehow implying a grievance.

"Mrs Hoolahan?" it repeated. "Well, I am Miss Mathew, housekeeper to Mr Magadoo, the District Justice."

Here it paused, as if to allow so weighty a piece of information to sink well in.

"Oh, how are you, I was going to ring up myself," said Grainne. "Only I hadn't a moment before. Is it about Mr Magadoo's case? We have it here. It's exactly like my husband's and it must be, they had them mixed. You probably have ours there."

"We have indeed," said Miss Mathew in sepulchral tones. "And let me say before anything else, I am more than sorry at what has occurred. I always unpack for Mr Magadoo in the usual way, but this time he wouldn't let me near, just belted upstairs and shut himself in his room."

Grainne had to smile at that, thinking of the poor man's disappointment.

"Well, I don't know that it was Brian's fault, really, when the cases were so alike," she said kindly. "I hope Mr Magadoo isn't too much annoyed."

"I cannot say if he is or not," the housekeeper tartly replied. "This minute, he is unconscious. As he never came down, I went up, and there he was, stretched on the bed like a corpse. There were several bottles of spirits in your husband's case, of which he seems to have emptied one. And they expecting him in Court tomorrow!"

Once again Grainne could feel the world collapsing all round her.

"Ah no, you can't mean it?" she cried in anguish. "And the pair of them fresh from St Paddy's!"

"Most unfortunate," Miss Mathew agreed, but with a kind of sinister relish. "And a disgrace to the country."

The stricture was so plainly intended for Brian that Grainne could not allow it to pass.

"There are four bottles of Scotch in Mr Magadoo's case, let me tell you," she retorted. "So now! It hardly mattered at all, which case he took."

A thin wailing cry of despair followed these words. Then, tremulously, the housekeeper asked in her turn: "Are you serious?"

"God Almighty, this isn't the time to be joking."

"What'll we ever do?" Miss Mathew whimpered. She was one of those Tartars that crumble easily.

"Take all the bottles and empty them out," Grainne replied without hesitation. "And neither of us will know a thing about them."

"That's a terrible liberty for me to be taking," Miss Mathew objected. "It's all very well for you. *I'm* a housekeeper, not a wife."

"Wife or housekeeper, neither of us will have seen or touched a bottle. D'you want the Justice inside again, before he's properly out?"

"Maybe you're right. I wonder, though, can I carry it off? Mr Magadoo will ask no end of questions. He's not a Justice for nothing."

At this point a violent altercation broke out in the hall below, with the Minister's voice easily riding the rest.

"Jesus and Mary, what is it now?" groaned his wife. "I'll have to let you go, Miss Mathew, this house is worse than Bedlam itself."

And without pausing to expand her statement or say goodbye, she quickly put the receiver down and hurried towards the scene of the new trouble.

ten

Grainne's first thought was, that the two old bosom friends
were having another row. Then, as she hastened downstairs, she saw from a landing window that the squad car
was still at the door, with only a driver in it. Startled, she
put on speed, to find the hall littered with scraps of paper,
Brian shouting over and over the name of Ruairí na Rigg
and struggling between two Guards, while a Sergeant and
Dr Macnamara attempted to calm him down. It looked as
if the Minister for Social Adjustment were resisting arrest;
but the truth was far from that and, if anything, worse.

These Guards were not a security patrol at all, but from
the city. Nor had they come to interview the Minister:

they wanted a word with Miss Nuala Hoolahan. Brian told them that she was out and asked the nature of their business, which at first they declined to reveal; but as the father, growing irate, insisted, reluctantly they gave way.

It appeared that, unknown to anyone else in the family, Nuala had twice been served with a summons to attend the Dublin District Court, and twice had failed to do so. The Guards had now brought a third and last invitation, and were instructed to say that if this too should be ignored, she would be arrested on indictment and charged, with the option of applying for bail.

"And she'd get it of course," the Sergeant assured the frantic parent. "That part of it's just a formality."

"But will you tell me what, in God's name, it is all about?" Brian stormed. A nice coming-home, to be sure. "Speeding? Parking?" A happy thought struck him and his fury died away. "It'll be political, I suppose," he said, smiling. "Sure, what would the young ones do, only fight against Ireland's wrongs?"

The Guards looked at each other in embarrassment, and the man in-charge gave the summons to Brian.

"The best is, you'll read it yourself," he said with a little cough.

Brian hastily opened the document and glanced through it, muttering a word here and there as he went along. His face took on an expression of utter bewilderment, and no sooner had he come to the end than he started all over again. Now the bewilderment slowly vanished and was followed by rage.

" '. . . did offer, advertise or expose for sale a contraceptive, contrary to Section 17 of the Criminal Law Amendment Act 1935 . . .' " he thundered. "Are you astray in your wits?"

But even as he spoke, he remembered the visit from

Ruairí na Rigg at St Padraig's, buried these many weeks in the depths of his mind.

"Ruairí na Rigg, Ruairí na Rigg! I'll get him for this!" he exploded. "The dirty double-dealing English bastard! Never trust the English!"

Here he was doing his colleague less than justice. The way in which Rigg had handled the matter was due indeed to the residual Englishman in him, but was wholly free of malice. He merely had seen no alternative. First, there had come the order to hush things up, and all the prisoners had been released. Then Dermot's article appeared, to make the hushing-up impracticable, and it was clear that charges would have to be preferred. But the Women's Lib contingent had all refused to give any names or addresses, so that there was now no tracing of them. Nuala was the only one involved on whom the authorities could lay their hands. The terrible dilemma thus posed was altogether too much for the minor officials who normally set the wheels of justice moving. It was referred to higher and higher powers until it landed on the desk of Ruairí na Rigg; and from that desk the barbarous Saxon-style command went forth, that the law must be upheld without respect of persons.

Brian tore the summons to shreds and flung these on the ground. Then he made a rush at the Sergeant, for want of Rigg himself. The other Guards moved in to the rescue and each grabbed one of the flailing arms, with muttered apologies and appeals, such as "Aisy now, Minister, aisy, aisy!"

"I'd never have wished it," the Sergeant protested. "I'm a father meself . . ."

"Arrah, Brian, will you quieten down?" said the doctor. "Till we talk this out."

Their combined endeavours merely threw oil on the flames. Although his arms were out of commission, Brian still had the wag of his tongue, and he burst into torrential abuse of the traitor Rigg and awful threats against his person. It was now that Grainne joined the group, entirely at sea as to what was up but prompt to defend her own.

"Will you let my husband go this minute? How dare you?" she cried; and then, as an afterthought, "What did he do?"

"Nothing at all, ma'am, nothing at all in the world," panted a Guard, putting a half-nelson on as Brian renewed his efforts to break away.

"Is that right? I'd be sorry, so, for the one that didn't," Grainne riposted. "Let him go, before you have him killed. He's only after coming from hospital. And what's the meaning of this at all?"

"Don't tell her!" Brian roared. "Unless you want to see her lying dead!"

"We came to see Miss Nuala Hoolahan on a little matter of business, ma'am, but she was out," the Sergeant said cautiously.

Grainne stared at him in horror. "The Yamaha!" she cried. "I was expecting this. Did she run anyone down?"

"Not at all. Nothing like that. Now, ma'am, we've done what we came for and we'll leave if the Minister lets us go. But please make sure the young lady is at the Bridewell, District Court number eight, at ten o'clock tomorrow."

At this, Dr Macnamara cleared his throat with an air of authority. "I say, she'll do no such thing," he said. "She is a patient of mine and she isn't fit."

This knightly intervention was typical of him. He was a man with the loftiest ideals in all that concerned his profession. As he saw it, his duty was not confined to diagnosing and physicking but required him to alleviate distress wherever it was found and to refuse no help of any description that he was able to bring. No one in need ever knocked at his surgery door in vain. He would certify sound as a bell, for insurance purposes, a man whose days he knew were numbered, or as perfectly sober, a captive in the cells who could barely stand or speak; and he would sign chits galore, recommending sick leave, for rugby fans anxious to attend a fixture in England or France. With Grellet, he might have said: 'I expect to pass through this world but once: any good thing therefore that I can do, or any kindness that I can show to any fellow-creature, let me do it now; let me not defer or neglect it, for I shall not pass this way again.'

The Sergeant shot him a piercing glance. "Would you be Dr Eoghen Macnamara of The Cedars, Dalkey, sir?" he wished to know.

"The very man," smiled the doctor, with a little innocent gratification at being thus widely known.

"We heard nothing as to the young lady's health on the previous occasions, sir," observed the Sergeant, still with that strange intensity of the eye.

"You would have heard fast enough, had I been aware of the matters pending." the doctor replied sonorously. "That Miss Hoolahan kept them from me, is entirely consistent with her depressive condition. Which of course I cannot discuss."

"We should require an affidavit from yourself," the other proceeded. "Are you ready to swear one?"

"By all means," the doctor assured him. "I will attend to it in the morning and forward it on."

"Very well, so," the Sergeant said, after a brief cogitation. The cards were too clearly stacked against him to pursue the inquiry further. "Of course, you'll understand that this merely means a postponement," he said to Brian, who had ceased struggling and shouting, and stood there dazed with his mouth open.

"Well, we were nicely conned at the finish," the Sergeant remarked as the squad car went down the drive. "So that was Macnamara. From the look of him, butter wouldn't melt in his mouth. Stop by at the Dalkey station, Tim. I want whoever watches that house to keep an eye on Miss Hoolahan."

"Could she not be examined by one of ours, Sarge?" asked Tim. "The doc would be in a fine mess then, with his affidavit. Enough to get him struck off."

"Ah, once you started striking off, there'd be no end to it. And who'd we find that was willing? In England now," the Sergeant went on with a sigh, "one lad gets up, and then another that flatly contradicts him, and the barristers go at it hammer and tongs till nobody knows if it's Christmas or Easter. This bloody country's too small. They all know each other, if they're not related as well, and they won't be annoying for fear of getting annoyed themselves one day."

Having delivered himself of these sombre reflections, he sank into a gloomy silence which lasted the whole of the way.

At Capri Heights, Grainne was vainly trying to learn the cause of the fracas. The doctor assured her that it was not worth a moment's thought: Nuala had been called as witness in a prosecution, and had neither appeared nor sent any excuse for her absence. If that was all, why was Brian so furious? and why were the Guards to tell her nothing? And what was this, Nuala was ill? She had never been so well in her life! And why did the Guards go for Brian? Or was it he went for them?

Deftly, the doctor parried her questions one by one.

"You'd best leave this to Brian and myself," he told her at last, with conscious masculine wisdom. "We have the matter under control, and there's no need in the world for dragging you in. Amn't I right, Brian boy?"

Brian had recovered his poise by now and was feeling a wish to assert himself. He fully approved Mac's sentiments and further reminded his wife that he was the man of the house; and with that the pair of them retired, with dignity, for one last smoke before the guest went home.

With men, however, it sometimes happens that for all their range of intellect, their vigorous grasp of essentials, they will overlook some minor but cogent detail; and this had happened here. The fragments of the summons still lay on the floor where the Minister had strewn them. Grumbling at the mess he always left for others to clear away, Grainne began to collect them up; and as it fell out, the very first scrap she took hold of bore the words 'for sale a contraceptive.'

For some moments she stared at it in horror. Then she gathered in all the rest and carried them off to the parlour, where she laboriously pieced the whole together again. As the work progressed, horror was piled on horror. It was like an infernal jigsaw puzzle. In all the disjointed phrases spread out before her, there was nothing about a witness. Here was a date—the date of her garden party! Where was the scrap that fitted next? She had it: 'you did offer, advertise or expose.' After that, in went neatly, 'for sale a contraceptive' . . . *Oh no!* But on she went. 'Whereas.' 'Whereof.' 'fail at your peril.' 'Criminal Law Amendm.' At last all was in place, the terrible content plain and unmistakable.

And yet, a mistake there must be. There was not one word of sense in it from start to finish. What would Nuala want with such dreadful things at all, let alone go hawking them round or advertizing them? Grainne knew nothing about the protest demo, because the day that Dermot's story appeared she had been wholly absorbed in searching for accounts of her party and had let the rest of the news go by. Before anything else, she decided, she would confront those two deceitful men and flatten them until they spoke the truth.

But putting that grisly mosaic together had taken time. The doctor was gone and the drawing-room empty, although the lights in it were burning still. It must be, Brian had gone to bed, leaving her, in his virile Irish way, to switch off, lock up and see to anything else that might require attention.

At this moment, however, the halldoor opened and Brian stumbled in, red of face and breathing hard.

"Is Nuala home?" Grainne opened fire.

"Don't know," he muttered vaguely, apparently wondering who she was. "Just took the dog for a walk."

She looked at him in angry despair. He must have been drinking, and heavily too, for the Hoolahans kept no dog. There was a dog at St Padraig's, where he doubtless supposed himself to be. It had been sheer criminal madness to let him out of her sight, whatever the reason. When Macnamara left, he would have gone upstairs to bed and come on those bottles in Magadoo's case. But nothing was to be gained by talking, with him in this condition.

"You'd best go on up and sleep it off," she said, in a tone of concentrated bitterness. "I just wonder, what Sister Lourdes would have to say, that's all."

Brian attempted to draw himself up, but soon abandoned the project, from a tendency to over-balance.

"Don't know what you mean," he managed, however, to assure her.

"Come along, I'll give you a hand."

This was how it ended, so, and would always end. When she got him upstairs and to bed, she looked in Magadoo's case. Every bottle of the four was gone, every last one. Well, she could do no more. It was all beyond her, too much for her slender powers. Sister Lourdes, Brian, Mac, the Guards, Nuala . . . She went to her daughter's room and then, finding no one there, downstairs again to wait up till whatever hour the child should deign to return.

As she reached the hall, Nuala came dancing in, looking her prettiest, and with a kind of radiance that seemed to transform her whole personality. The questions that Grainne had prepared died away on her lips. She smiled wanly, told her her father was tired and had gone to bed and hoped she had spent a good evening. At most she expected a perfunctory word or two and a hasty goodnight kiss; but to her amazement, Nuala rushed up and threw her arms round her neck.

"Oh Mummy, Mummy, you'll never guess!" she cried. "This is the happiest day of my life!" And with that she showered kisses on her thunder-struck parent as if she never meant to stop.

"Tell you all tomorrow!" she said at last. "Just now I need my beauty sleep!" Half jumping, half dancing, she tore away upstairs, leaving Grainne's mind in more of a whirl than ever.

eleven

It sometimes will happen that pieces of luck come falling out of the blue, investing life for the time being with the charm of a fairy story; and such was Nuala's experience now. Grainne had noted her frequent absence from home in the holiday period, but put it down to mild dislike of her brothers and sisters and positive loathing of their children. She had noted too, could hardly fail to note, that she was much less moody, resentful and snubbing than usual but, interpreting incorrectly again, thought this due to happiness in her engagement.

The truth was as different as could be. One evening in a bar, Dermot had introduced her to a man who made brief commercials for showing on Telefís Eireann. He, after looking her over and up and down with undisguised approval, asked if she would care to try her hand at these. The money was good, he told her, and the demands on the intellect by no means heavy. All she had to do was crack up some product or other, accompanying the words with an imbecile grin in the case of food or a knowing leer for cosmetics or scent.

Nuala allowed herself to be persuaded, although she had certain misgivings. Like many young girls, she had often dreamed of becoming an actress, but this was a most inferior branch of dramatic art. And her parents would not like it at all: there might be trouble at home. But Dermot pointed out that, on the rare occasions when they watched the telly, it was always the BBC: the chances were all against their even knowing. So it was agreed; and shortly afterwards she made her debut, a winsome colleen in a long green skirt, puffing a brand of Irish lard as if the health of the nation depended on their using this and rejecting all other.

It was here that the luck began. In this, her very first appearance, she caught the eye of a real producer, a giant of a man, who brought out the big dramatic features. He was at present working on one more protracted serial of simple family life in an Irish village, and he saw at once that Nuala's looks would help to brighten it up, as was sorely needed. He found out who she was, fixed an audition and, realizing that she had some talent, immediately offered her a small part as the best-loved nun in the local convent school.

This was stupendous fortune indeed, and she threw herself into the rôle with might and main. Her whole-hearted identification with it, in fact, was behind the unwonted sweetness towards the family circle which had surprised and gratified Grainne during the holidays. But greater things yet were in store. The principal young female character was that of a girl who had shaken off the noise, bustle and paganism of London and returned to the quiet Christian place of her birth where, after ups and downs spinning out over a year or two, she would marry a rich young farmer. And now, a bare fortnight before the initial episode was to be played, the actress who took this part had received an offer from ITV and, mindless of her contract, deaf to remonstrance and entreaty, had legged it to that same noisy, bustling pagan city with all the speed she could muster! And Nuala, Nuala Hoolahan, the little inexperienced rosebud who had only appeared in end-of-term plays at the Bambino Gesú, and these as a rule by Lady Gregory, was invited to take her place!

It was this that brought her home treading on air, too excited even to break the news, and kept her unable to sleep or lie down, sitting for hours by her window and looking over the sea. As with people in love, the world was suddenly born again and she felt kindly towards everything in it. And not the least remarkable instance of change was the view she now took of the forthcoming serial. When it had been announced, she had groaned, "What, another?" It would be corny, dull, a feeble imitation of the BBC, and the characters just as before with different names.

There would have to be the benevolent parish priest—no escaping *him*! Scheming farmer with his eye on somebody's piece of land. Good farmer, always helping his neighbours out. Unmarried female gossip. Devoted smiling nuns, with a solitary pickle-puss among them as a daring touch of realism. Problem teenager. Amusing old drunk, full of quaint and unnaturally erudite maxims. Rowdy itinerants. And the heroine, of course, renouncing a brilliant career abroad and settling down to happy Christian marriage with an honest farmer and—although these would of course not have time to appear—thirteen children.

Her prognostication in fact was entirely correct, as Bracken the producer knew to his grief. He would have liked nothing better than to give a glimpse of the real thing, and most of the viewers would have hailed it with joyful mirth. Graft, incompetence, inertia, bribes, fixes, wealth mysteriously acquired, scandals hushed up, records conveniently lost if kept at all, servants of the people a-fishing or a-drinking in office hours and, along of all this, that nothing would ever be done—why, Gogol was nowhere! It was novelty, not morality, that he was pining for and rich indeed was the spread that lay below, should anyone dare take the lid off. But no one would, for two excellent reasons: first, the uproar that would burst from the parties involved, and second, the policy of Telefís Eireann, which was to regale the public—and especially any foreigners knocking about—with an 'image' of the country so artfully touched and retouched as to be all but unrecognizable. And so, with resignation, Bracken prepared once more to plod along the familiar path.

Nuala, on the other hand, had now revised her opinions entirely. It was going to be the most gorgeous serial ever screened, putting *The Forsyte Saga* in the shade and consigning *The Pallisers* to oblivion. She explained as much to Grainne early next morning, finding her up and alone, and fairly bubbled over with the immensity of her prospects, the money, the fame, people looking after her in the street and pointing out Nuala Hoolahan!

"Well, you'd better learn to milk a cow and set potatoes," was her mother's first reaction. "The last time I saw those jackeens at it, I nearly died laughing."

"And is that all you have to say?" demanded the indignant artist. "Aren't you one little bit proud of me?"

"I am, of course," Grainne hastily assured her. "Only I didn't quite take it in as yet."

"They'll sell it to America and I'll be better known than Jackie Onassis!"

This promise of glory brought to Grainne's mind the troubling events of the previous night. "I don't know, would your father and I want that," she said hesitantly, wondering how to go on.

"Mummy, you look quite solemn! And I thought you'd be as thrilled as I am. Don't tell me that acting is sinful now, like all the other pleasures!"

"I'm thrilled all right." But Grainne did not sound it. "Nuala, childeen, are you in some kind of trouble? The Guards were round yesterday evening . . ."

"The Guards, the Guards!" Nuala broke in, tossing her hair back. "Don't mind them."

"But they seemed to think you'd done something dreadful."

"Well, they're wrong, so now. I don't know what we pay them for. They mixed me up with those creatures in the demo."

"Demo? what demo?" Grainne inquired, in growing bewilderment.

"Ah, Mummy, d'you ever read the paper?" asked Nuala with a theatrical groan. "That day I went to Belfast, your party day in the summer, there was a crowd of Women's Lib on the train and at Connolly, all demonstrating, waving contraband stuff and offering it for sale. The Guards supposed I must be with them and took my name. I didn't tell you, you'd only be upset for nothing. The Guards sent me a summons or two, but Dermot said there was no case to answer, and I tore them up."

Grainne looked at her thoughtfully, noting the uneasiness behind the fluent delivery of this speech. That uneasiness was merely due to Nuala's having forgotten the precise events themselves and not yet wholly believing the amended version proposed by Dermot. After a few more rehearsals she would vividly recall, see again in her mind's eye, every detail of that version and be prepared, with absolute calm, to recite it on her oath; for the process whereby myth hardens to fact in the Irish mind is sure, if sometimes slow.

"They wanted you in the District Court number eight at ten this morning," her mother said. "But Dr Macnamara stepped in like a decent skin and told them you were ill. He's going to send in an affidavit."

"And what business of his was that? These old men and their affidavits!" Nuala spoke as if affidavits were a disorder connected with age. "The last thing I want just now is a rumour that I'm ill. I'll go to the silly old Court, so, and let them know there what I think."

"But the papers! It'll be in the papers!" Grainne cried.

"Amn't I telling you, I did nothing at all and the case will be thrown out? Most likely I'll get compensation. And it's good publicity."

In Grainne's eyes, no publicity of this nature could ever be good; but nothing she could say had the least effect, and Nuala rushed off to get ready for a trip to the Bridewell.

Brian was still sleeping his potions off, and Geraldine so far had not appeared. As Grainne set about her daily chores, her spirit grew quiet and even joyful. There was no doubt of it, Nuala had more pluck than the rest of the family put together. It was like her to face the music now, and she'd best them all, and the wretched business would be finished and done. The worry of it was what had started Brian drinking again, and soon they could tell him it was all over. *Mother of God, make it so, and I'll go to Knock* . . . And Nuala's amazing good fortune also began to warm her heart, as the fullness of it slowly sank in. They couldn't have found her a better part, come to that, the girl preferring Ireland to ease and wealth and comfort, what with her own father, the Minister, working away like mad to bring the exiles home.

She was smiling to herself, thinking how bright the future looked after all, when there came a knock at the hall-door. Answering it, she found Lady Belling's gardener, who handed her an envelope with a coronet on the back.

"For you, mum, from her ladyship," he said, respectfully lifting his cap. "She didn't say, was there an answer expected."

"I can ring her up, if necessary," Grainne said, all in a flutter. She could feel that the envelope contained a card. Could it be, must it not be, an invitation to some brilliant gathering, among the titled, rich and elegant?

Overwhelmed by Lady Belling's complaisance in attending her party, Grainne at first had looked for no return. That her ladyship had stood on the lawn at Capri Heights and been visible to all other guests there, was emolument enough. Then as time went on and no word of any description, not even a thank-you, came from the Castle, her familiar demon started muttering in her ear. She had been slighted, passed over, she was good enough—just—to issue invitations but not so grand as to be invited back. Her family were sated with accounts, growing wilder with every repetition, of the woman's rudeness over the Soldier's Song.

But now with that card in her hand, all resentment died away in a flash. She carried it off to a quiet place indoors, as a dog carries a bone, and tore it from its wrapping. Die-stamped across the top were the words FROM: MAUDE, LADY BELLING, CASTLE TRIG, CO DUBLIN, and it expressed no desire for her presence at any function at all. In a manly sprawling script, it went as follows:

To Mrs Hoolahan.

I should be more than grateful if you, or your husband, would not shy empty bottles over my garden wall. Last night while I was exercising Bimbo four of them came over in quick succession and one of them hit him on the nose. He could have been blinded. My gardener informs me that this is no unusual occurrence.

M.B.

That was all, a terse admonition from someone far above to another far below, with the insolence of rank in every line. Lady Belling might never have been to her house, never have quaffed her wine nor munched her frosted cakes. She here addressed herself as to a total stranger. And the very idea, that anyone in Capri Heights would throw bottles over a neighbour's wall, like a pack of tinkers! Grainne felt ready to burst with rage; but the moment after she realized that this was exactly what had occurred, and by the Minister's hand. He had poured as much of the liquor as he had not yet swallowed into some capacious receptacle—probably one of the Japanese vases that she was so proud of—and staggered forth in the darkness to dispose of the incriminating containers. It was Bimbo's yelp of pain, no doubt, that led him to fancy he was up at St Padraig's, strolling through the grounds with Sinbad the Sailor.

But before anything else, she must find that cache of liquor. It would be the first thing he would look for, once he woke up. She could hear Geraldine moving about in the kitchen now, and was almost tempted to recruit her in the search; but the shame of it would kill her. She peered into each of the Japanese vases, one either side of the stairway, but they were empty. Where could it be? Not in the parlour, for she had been there herself, piecing that abominable summons together. Not in the drawing room, either, for there was nothing there that would hold it unless he removed the pepper-tree from its pot, and then there would be no concealing it. Could he have hidden it somewhere in the bedroom, when he took the bottles from the case? but she had smelt nothing spirituous, apart from his breath, all night, and the various pitchers and basins had all been in order.

Brian could not have drunk it all or he would surely be dead. Some three pints must be left, which could not simply evaporate. The crafty ruses of alcoholics were infinite, as she knew; and it struck her that the best, though humbling, course was now to consult Sister Lourdes, whose tales of their strategems, artifices and diabolical ingenuities would have comfortably lasted the thousand and one nights, or longer.

She moved towards the library to make her call on the separate line, her steps dragging, her heart sick with this new and deadly mortification. From the kitchen came a piercing shriek, which, like a factory whistle, blew daily as the signal that Geraldine was there and the kettle for her morning tea had come to the boil. But that daily shriek always calmed to a hollow mutter as Geraldine took the kettle off. This continued in a series of earsplitting blasts, like those of a train as it enters a tunnel, until Grainne realized they must proceed from the woman herself.

She ran to the kitchen and flung open the door, to be confronted by an amazing sight. The whole top of the Aga was swept with dancing blue flames, such as gaily leap round a Christmas pudding, continually supplemented by furious spurts from the kettle. The pleasant fragrance of burning malt permeated the room.

"Don't go nigh it, woman dear, the devil's in it," Geraldine bawled, her professional animosity suspended. "I filled that kettle from the tap, last thing before I went home. It must be this new infanticide they put through the water now, to kill the germs that's in it. Well, they've surely taken years off me life, and it's the Water Board will have to pay me . . ."

Grainne seized an ovencloth and moved the fuming kettle to a colder place, where it continued to rumble and hiss like a volcano between eruptions, while the flames kept up their antic dance like an army of will-o'-the-wisps.

"Don't mind them, they'll soon burn out," Grainne soothed her domestic, who sank into a chair and threw her apron over her head. "Some boys came in, and they were for making punch. They'll have thrown the water out and put the spirits there instead." Ah, but what wouldn't she say to Brian!

This explanation brought Geraldine to herself faster than a bucket of water over her face. Removing her apron, she felt in the pocket for a smoke, lit it and, fixing a baleful eye on her mistress, spoke as follows, while the cigarette wagged up and down.

"Nice company you keep, then," she barked, belligerent. "This place is what I'd call a death-trap. I'm giving me notice, Gracie Hoolahan, and God help all that come after me."

Her effrontery all but took Grainne's breath away. Gracie Hoolahan! Not even 'Grainne,' which Gaelic form of that name she had assumed when Brian went into politics.

"Whatever you like yourself," she said, almost relieved, as the eternal inner debate as to whether Geraldine was better than nothing or not could now be concluded. "But while you're here, just mind your manners."

The ring of the telephone bell allowed her to make a suitable exit on this speech, and she swept superbly out.

"Manners, is it?" cackled Geraldine after her retreating form. "There's more than manners need minding at Crappy Heights!"

Ignoring this further impudence, Grainne went to answer the call. Nuala's pretty voice, gayer than ever, came lilting down the line.

"Everything's OK, Mummy, what did I tell you?" she said. "I'm ringing from the Court-house now. Case dismissed. All over and done with. They hadn't a leg to stand on! Can't stop, I'm off to rehearsal. Just wanted you to know." And with that she hung up.

Grainne sat for a while, fondling the receiver as if it were a well-loved child. The sun had burst through the clouds, as it so often did when the sky looked its blackest. Nuala had triumphed over the evil forces conspiring against her, and the family honour was safe. The missing liquor was found, would be disposed of, and Brian should get no more. The one jarring note was that impudent message from the woman next door, and this she would answer without delay. No admissions or apologies were in contemplation, but a stern rejoinder, as to an unfounded and intolerable charge. It was unfortunate that she had no printed cards like those of Lady Belling, the very use of which seemed to take the recipient down a peg; but she would reply on Brian's official paper, with the embossed harp and the address all in Irish, issued only to members of the ruling class.

Taking a sheet of this, she wrote swiftly,

From: Grainne Mrs Hoolahan. To: Lady Belling.

But after that came a long pause. Nothing she could think of, pleased her. She longed to assume the cutting lapidary style of the original, but only managed to sound querulous, aggrieved and offensive. Draft after draft she composed, and tore them up in angry frustration. Finally,

however, she knocked something out which would show
Lady B. the Hoolahans were not to be bullied:

*I assure you, any empty bottles in this house are collected
by the leading vintner who supplies us. The idea of my husband or me throwing them over your wall is abserd. Those
that came over last night were probably pitched by some
trespasing boy. This neighburhood is not what it was.*

G.H.

She read it over and over and liked it better every time.
Having made a neat copy, she sent it to the post, having no
gardener to act as go-between, and smiled to herself as she
imagined Lady Belling's discomfiture.

Lady Belling chuckled over the orthography, but was
otherwise wholly unmoved.

"Those bottles you collected for me, Fergus," she said to
her gardener. "Shy them back where they came from, and
any others you can find. And have a good look round, to
see if they've dumped any rubbish on us. Civility is wasted
on these people. All tinkers at heart."

twelve

Three summonses to appear before the District Court had been served on Nuala Hoolahan. Or, to be exact, one summons had been served three times, on the second and third of which there was added and threatening material as to eventualities if she continued to ignore it. They should rightly then have alarmed her more on each occasion; but such was not the case.

It was the first one that threw her into panic. She had never seen a document of this nature before and it struck her as excessively disagreeable. Worse, it arrived just as Liam left and the other family visits would follow on. Nothing else would be in anyone's mind until every last one had departed. There would be icy comment from Fr Matt, fiery denunciation from Sister Dolours, among the others an unspoken agreement to behave as if she were invisible, with Grainne either prostrate or in hysterics most of the day. She would be excluded from the family Mass on Sunday and the family rosary at night. The charge against her, indeed, was untrue, but the truth was worse; and whatever the outcome of the case, the mere fact of its being brought and noted in the Press would be shame and horror enough. She would be the black sheep of the family, instead of as heretofore its pride and joy, the 'real lady' it somehow had contrived to throw up and before whom it bowed in homage.

In tearing the summonses to pieces and burning them, her intention was simply to gain a little time. Once the family, that many-headed monster, had vacated the house, there would be only Grainne to contend with, who might be brought to a state of mental confusion where she hardly knew who was charged with what. Nuala realized the summons would come again, and so it did; but, from its own point of view, it chose a singularly ill-judged moment, the very day of Nuala's audition with Bracken, when nothing else in the world had any real importance.

She stuffed it in the Aga without a qualm.

Now it was here again, and again with a poor sense of timing. At the very moment that her father was scattering the fragments about the floor and howling for the Sergeant's blood, she was with Bracken in Davy Byrnes's bar, being offered the leading rôle in the new series. When she got home, it was to find that all she had dreaded over the months had come to pass. Her father knew, her mother knew, and in no time the family network would go into action. But she suddenly saw that it no longer mattered. The circumstances of her life were radically changed. She would cock a snook at the whole lot. And what was this all-powerful ogre-family, take it piece by piece? Alcoholic father, one brother ditto, mother with her holy beads and snobbisms and her cherished Infant of Prague, that she didn't even know the origin of but vaguely supposed He brought money into the house, Matt still a curate, Dolours with a moustache and beard that she offered up instead of having it treated, and the rest with nothing in their brains but making money and spawning children!

These were heady thoughts for a young woman who, barely nine months ago, had quitted the Bambino Gesù with an illumined parchment bearing witness to her exemplary conduct and notable Catholic formation. And now, as she raced along the highway on the Yamaha, came others that were stranger still, in fact unheard-of, world-shaking and revolutionary. Why, when she got into Court, should she not tell the truth? Why pitch this yarn of having the stuff planted on her, that no one in any case would ever believe? Why not frankly state that what she bought in Belfast was of no concern to anyone but herself? She had broken no law and intended to break none. The goods were for her own use and it was between herself and her conscience. Would that not strike a more resounding blow for freedom than all those shrieking Women's Libbers rolled into one? It was time to put an end to this hole-and-corner way of life, with everyone saying one thing and doing another. The younger people and the more intelligent of the older would all be on her side; and she would be a national heroine, which was the most attractive argument of all.

Now she came to the outskirts of Dublin, and accordingly reduced her speed to the rush-hour crawl. Her thoughts went racing on, however, and even the squat figure of the Bridewell with blue cars nosing up to it or away, or looping it like a cumbersome necklace, did nothing to check them. She parked the motor-bicycle, was commanded to move it, and parked it elsewhere with the same result.

"I'm leaving it here," she told the Garda with spirit, "or taking it into Court." And without waiting for his reaction, she tripped off in search of number eight.

They showed her into a dismal waiting-room across the passage from the Court itself. It was already thronged with people, a motley crew, thieves, vagrants, streetwalkers, motorists, some looking dejected, others defiant or brazen, talking nervously or indignantly to their legal advisers. Guards came and went, calm and detached as keepers at the Zoo. The fatherly man who had betrayed her at the Customs bench walked in with a file under his arm and looked vaguely through her as if they had never met before.

"Nuala Hoolahan!" a voice exclaimed in her ear. Turning, she was confronted by a former classmate, Petra Slieve, a star pupil herself and fellow recipient of the coveted *honoris causa* scroll. "Fancy meeting you here! Is it your first time?"

"Yes," Nuala said, as surprised by the encounter as Petra was. "Is it yours?"

"No, indeed," Petra replied; and in fact she had the air of one thoroughly at home. "Shop-lifting, you know. I can't think why they make such a fuss about it," she continued fretfully. "With things the price they are, what on earth are people to do? You're the same, I suppose?"

"No," Nuala said frigidly, drawing aside from the shameless girl with marked disapproval.

"Don't tell me! Let me guess! Marijuana?"

Nuala shook her head, and turned away.

"If it's some dreary old parking offence, I'll have nothing to do with you," Petra giggled, refusing to be snubbed. "Let me see. Not shop-lifting, not marijuana. Not political, or you'd be at Green Street. I know—drinking after hours!"

But here they were interrupted by an official, with a list in his hand.

"Nuala Hoolahan, of Capri Heights?" he asked. "Why didn't you present your summons at the door?"

"My father tore it up."

"She's the one I was telling you of," a Sergeant called out. "We understood you were ill, miss."

"Well, I am not, as you see." To a further question, she answered no, she was not represented and did not intend to be. "There's no case to answer. I haven't broken the law."

"That is as may be," the official said. "I'd best have a word with the Clerk of the Court. Stay here till I raise him."

By this time Petra was all agog. "You'll have to tell me after all, I could never guess," she said, her eyes shining. "Were you going to blow up the Customs House? No one can think why it hasn't been done, with the Lion and the Unicorn all over the place. Much worse than Nelson."

"I would love to blow it up all right, and everyone in it," Nuala said bitterly. "I brought back some contraceptives from Belfast and they took them off me at Connolly station. And now they're making out, I was going to sell them."

"Jesus, Mary and Joseph!" Petra gasped, turning crimson and recoiling, as Nuala had done from her own disclosures. "But what could you be wanting with such things?"

"To use them, of course. Or did you think, 'twas to flavour the soup?"

Petra stared at her in horror, hardly able to believe what she heard. "But it's murder," she brought out at length. "What would Reverend Mother say?"

"And what would she say to your picking and stealing?"

"We don't call it that," Petra replied, affronted. "It is a simple matter of adjustment and distribution."

"Well, it's landed you here, whatever you call it."

"I'm ashamed of you, downright ashamed to be seen with you!" Petra declared in ringing tones. "An Irish Catholic girl! It wouldn't surprise me one bit if that scroll the Infant Jesus gave you didn't turn black. I always wondered, how you got it."

But this exchange of opinion now had to close, as the official returned with the Clerk of the Court, an amiable portly gentleman who seemed about as concerned as if Nuala had lost an umbrella.

"You should have a solicitor, Miss Hoolahan," he began at once. "You will want someone of experience, to advise you how to plead."

"I'm going to plead not guilty, which is what I am," Nuala said. "I had nothing to do with that demo that was offering things for sale. I never saw one of those women before in my life."

The Clerk smiled and stroked his ample chin. "Quite so," he said kindly. "But what's a demo these days, even an illegal one? High-spirited young people—misguided, of course," he put in hastily. "Whereas the alternative . . . have you considered that?"

"The alternative is something the law allows."

"But public opinion, Miss Hoolahan, public opinion!" cried the Clerk, showing a trace of emotion at last. "Have you any idea of the fury of public opinion in Ireland? Whereas the law. . . !"

But nothing he could say had the least effect.

Now a little stir ran through the room. The Justice had arrived and was about to take his seat. The Clerk had to hurry away to attend to his regular duties. From the courtroom across the passage, the buzz of voices died away and there was scraping and shuffling as people rose to their feet. This was followed by a mysterious crash; and then there came more shuffling as the people sat down again.

"May I take this opportunity of welcoming your Worship back to his Court?" Nuala heard someone say.

"Eh, whazzat?" came in a vague mutter. "Oh, thanks very much. Much obliged to you all."

This morning, the first back at duty, Justice Magadoo was not at the height of his powers. Like many of his race, he clung to a myth that the sovereign remedy for over-indulgence the night before was a plentiful draught of fiery liquid early in the morning. That remedy he had applied, omitting his breakfast to give it a freer run; but the effect was like that of petrol splashed on to red-hot cinders. Far from clearing his head, it piled extra confusion on what was already there; and his efforts to bring this under control was hampered by what seemed to be a carillon of ill-assorted bells. Even before he fell into his chair, those watching his erratic gait feared that his judgements might lose in clarity what they might conceivably gain in *fougue*.

Another difficulty faced him, none of his making and which he could not have foreseen. What with his long absence and the general easing-off in summer, it had been decided to take the opportunity of redecorating the courtroom. Instead of the soft blue chamber he was accustomed to, he found himself in one of a cruel restless pink. It all added to the sense of nightmare that oppressed him, and he began to wonder if he should last out the day. But with an effort he pulled himself together and bethought him of the cardinal rules in a situation like this—for it was by no means the first—namely, to take complete control, keep everyone to the point and avoid abstruse legal arguments as far as he could.

"Well, here we are," he observed. "We may as well begin."

What with the summons getting torn up and an affidavit in prospect, Nuala had been placed at the head of the list in case she slipped through their fingers after all. Her name was cried and she was ushered into the dock, where she stood, head held high, looking about her with queenly disdain. A solicitor rose to his feet, consulted a paper and began: "Is your name Nuala Hoolahan and do you reside at the house named Capri Heights in the County of Dublin?"

These were the very type of superfluous questions that the Justice did not propose to allow.

"Of course it is, and of course she does," he broke in abruptly. "We all know that. Try and come to the point."

"Your Worship . . ."

"Don't waste the Court's time, Mr Burke. Carry on, if you please." Mr Burke threw a martyred glance at the ceiling, and read out the charge with laboured distinctness. The Justice looked at him fixedly over his spectacles, thinking the man beside him must be a twin, they were so oddly alike.

"Do you plead guilty or not guilty?" Mr Burke then inquired.

"Not guilty," Nuala replied, with a toss of her hair.

"Quite right too," said the Justice. "I could have told you that, Mr Burke, but you must always have your say. Case dismissed."

"But your Worship has not heard the evidence!" cried Mr Burke, dramatically flinging his paper down on the desk.

"Did you, or did you not, hear the accused tell us that she was not guilty?" asked the Justice. "Then what purpose would be served by ploughing through all the evidence? It is that kind of senseless repetition which brings the law into disrepute."

"But there are witnesses to be called . . ."

"You should have considered that before," said the Justice incisively. "If you solicitors would get your cases up properly, it would save a deal of time and public money.

No more argument, please, or I shall ask you to stand down."

The legal men looked at each other in despair, while the reporters wrote industriously, and the Gardai did their best not to laugh. There had been odd happenings with the Justice before today, but never on such a scale as this; and no one could think what to do.

"Your Worship . . ." resumed the indomitable Burke.

"The case is dismissed, Mr Burke. How often must I speak? The accused may leave the dock at once, without a stain on her character."

"Thank you, your Worship," Nuala said, and hurried away before anyone could find some objection. Undoubtedly, it was an anticlimax, but a most agreeable one. "Case dismissed," she mockingly informed Petra on the way out. "And not a stain on my character!"

"Then I tremble for Ireland," was the tragic reply.

Back in the court-room they were proceeding, or endeavouring to proceed, with the next case. The accused now was none other than the bowsie man from the Gaeltacht. It was so long since he broke out last that Dublin had assumed his campaign was abandoned as fruitless: in fact, he had been lifting potatoes in Scotland, his custom at this time of year. That seasonal occupation over, he had emerged Lazarus-like from the shadows and left a trail of destruction all over the city.

Mr Burke stopped fanning his brow with the indictment, rose to his feet again and wearily announced: "Your Worship, this man refuses to give his name."

"I daresay he has his reasons," Justice Magadoo replied, as one always ready to believe the best of people. Having disposed of case number one so adroitly, his confidence was returning. "He may not remember it. I'm very apt to forget my own."

Mr Burke leaned with both hands on his desk and

bowed his head, as if seeking help from a Higher Power. Then, looking up, "I am asking your Worship," he said hoarsely, "for a declaration that the accused is mute of malice and . . ."

Here the bowsie man burst into an angry roar. "He is, in me eye," he barked. "I don't recognize the Court, and that's all about it."

"Nor do I!" the Justice exclaimed with fervour. "Who ever could?"

His words led to an unfortunate misunderstanding. They referred to nothing but the fierce pink paint on the walls, which had afflicted his hot, aching eyes from the moment he entered the room. But he uttered them with such vehemence that they rolled off his tongue like the traditional defiant cry of Sinn Fein: he seemed, bizarrely, to refuse recognition to the very Court over which he himself was presiding. That, at least, was the sense in which Mr Burke interpreted them; and he concluded that the Justice was not merely drunk but insane.

It was undoubtedly a delicate situation, and one for which Mr Burke could recall no precedent to guide him. In this particular matter, he could ask for an adjournment while the Gardai made further inquiries about the accused; but what of the cases to follow? How could justice be done, and seen to be done, with Magadoo in his present frame of mind?

"I crave your Worship's indulgence for a moment," he said, with a respectful bow, and skipped across to the Clerk of the Court.

"Micky," he muttered, "Old Kevin is crackers."

"I agree," whispered the Clerk.

"We have to stop this somehow. The Court must be cleared."

"And how the devil are we going to do that?"

"Bomb scare."

"Bomb scare!"

Mr Burke's solution was the bold and simple kind to be expected of him. For some time past, irritated perhaps by themselves or their property being steadily blown up over the years, certain Protestants in the North had embarked on a policy of tit for tat; and to meet this peril an alarm had been installed in every official building throughout the Republic. The nation had been apprised through the media of what they had to do in the event of its sounding: namely, to remain perfectly cool and carry out the orders of those in charge. The alarm, Mr Burke decided, should now be given, and the officer to whom the task was entrusted should return with a message purporting to give the whereabouts of the bomb. This would be placed before the Justice—and if that didn't sober him, what could?—and he would then direct the immediate evacuation of the Court.

This was the outcome envisaged in the tidy legal brain of Mr Burke; but nothing went according to plan. At the first lugubrious banshee howl of the siren, everyone except Justice Magadoo, the Clerk and Mr Burke fled precipitately from the room, yelling, jostling and calling on their Maker. The bowsie man headed the flight and was seen no more.

"What is the meaning of this outrage?" thundered the Justice, banging the table before him with both clenched fists.

"There . . . there appears to be a bomb scare, your Worship," said Mr Burke, lamely.

"Bomb scare fiddlesticks! There's been no alarm." For the Justice supposed the siren to be but a late-comer to the concerto inside his head. "Football result, more likely. Once and for all, I will not have my Court turned into a pantomime, or a menagerie either. This is the thanks I get for resuming my duties against my doctor's advice. Very well, I adjourn *sine die*. Adjourn, adjourn. Be off, the two of you."

And with that he lay back in his chair and composed himself for sleep.

And so the people of Dublin never thrilled to the clarion cry for truth, sincerity and straight dealing contemplated by Miss Nuala Hoolahan. She did not figure in the news at all. The complex matters of the day boiled down to a few brief lines: "An alarm was sounded in Dublin District Court No. 8 this morning but was traced to a fault in the wiring. All concerned, officials, Gardai and public, displayed an exemplary self-control and perfect order was maintained."

thirteen

Work on the forthcoming re-portrayal of simple Irish life
had broken off for lunch, and Bracken the producer con-
ducted his new leading lady to the Hunting Lodge at the
Gresham: the venue, as he underlined, was made possible
by a stroke of luck on the Turf rather than the bounty of
Telefís Eireann.

"You're going to be great," he assured her, over the
smoked salmon. "You have just that dewy innocence about
you that one only finds in Ireland. How did you get on this
morning, by the way?"

He laughed so much at the flounderings of Justice Magadoo that he nearly choked. "Isn't it a thousand pities, one

can never show things as they are?" he asked ruefully, when he was able to speak again. "A scene like that would be a riot. But then we'd all be out of a job, and on our way to England."

Pleased with the success of her recital, Nuala thought she would share the cream of the joke with him.

"The best of it was, I was going to spill the beans," she said. "And the Justice never gave me a chance to do it!"

"Beans?" queried Bracken. "What beans? Weren't you to say the stuff was planted on you, and stick to that?"

"That was Dermot's idea," she replied, with a wave of her hand that dismissed him. "But I had a better. I was going to tell them, loud and clear, that the stuff was mine and the law allowed me to have it. I was going to make them all sit up!"

Bracken leaned back in his chair and gazed at her. "D'you really mean what you're saying?"

"Of course I do."

"Well, then, thank all the saints in heaven for Justice Magadoo!"

Now it was Nuala's turn to be amazed. She had taken a strong liking to Bracken, and not simply on account of what he had done for her. He appeared so free in his mind, not cynical like Dermot, but unprejudiced, unshockable, one to whom you could say whatever came into your head. She had never known such a person before. All her life, with family, teachers, friends, there had been the eternal web of evasion, half-truth or downright fib, as if the function of words was to act as a protective covering. At last, she believed, she had found someone different—and here he was, goggling at her as it might have been her own mother!

"I thought you would be all for it," she said with a little tremor in her voice, like a hurt child.

"And so I am, of course. An end to all the make-believe

—haven't I said it a hundred times? But, me dear thing, if you had done that, you could never be in our show. I wouldn't be let employ you."

"So we are to be hypocrites for ever," was the dismal reply. Really, Bracken sounded like the Clerk of the Court!

He laughed. " 'For ever' is strong talk," he said. "But you must give us time—say, a couple of thousand years."

"Someone will have to make a start somewhere."

"Well, for the love of all that's holy, don't let it be you. The very idea gives me the shivers. Just when I've found the Ideal Irish Girl! If you ever feel tempted that way again, read the correspondence in the Press."

He spoke good sense. The Dáil was sitting again and, ingenious as it always was in delaying, sidetracking or finally shelving whatever promised trouble, it really looked as if something of some nature would soon have to be, if not done, at any rate considered. This led to the daily bombardment of the Press by citizens resolved that Ireland should not go to the dogs for lack of advice from them. For the most part, their effusions merely repeated, with varying degrees of ferocity, the old familiar arguments; but what gave them such interest as they had was, that all were written by those whom the matter least concerned. The fieriest advocates of unlimited birth were priests, nuns and pious laymen, except for here and there a mother of thirteen or so, grimly resolved that others should not escape. The silence of married women, possibly due to their hands being full enough as it was, lent the discussion a curious air of unreality; but the contumely heaped on dissenters was sufficiently real to deter all but the most intrepid.

"And take that 'Mammy has but a few more months to live' off your face," he teased her. "I shan't want it till January at the earliest. Let's have that glow of ecstasy you put on this morning. 'How do I feel, coming home to Ireland?

I could bow down and kiss the earth.' Anyone would swear you meant it!''

This timely reference to her attainments had the desired result. The glow reappeared in Nuala's face forthwith and the pair of them finished the meal in high spirits before resuming work in the studio. After that Nuala went off to meet Dermot, whom she had not yet told of her news, expecting to be overwhelmed with fervid congratulations.

She found him in a difficult mood, remote, distrait, seeming hardly to listen when she spoke. He had a number of troubles just then and was disinclined to rejoice at another's success, let alone the success of one whom he regarded as a mere appendage of himself.

First, there was the sensational affair of the *Globe*. With the return of the Board from their holidays, the matter of the Bishop of Killygobragh could no longer be deferred. The more they humbled themselves, pleaded their innocence and dwelt on the miseries they had to endure from the Printers' Union, the more obdurate and indeed voracious the Bishop grew. In his heated imagination, the affair had assumed the shape of a Holy War between the forces of righteousness, himself, and those of the Devil, the printers. And things, from his point of view, were running nicely. The Chairman, directors and Fergus O'Grady could see no help for it but humiliating, expensive, old-fashioned collapse.

Their solicitors were actually at work on the relevant document, carefully putting the traditional fulsome phrases together, when the bombshell struck. The Bishop was directed—not asked, invited, coaxed, but directed!—by higher authority to abandon the action, resign from his diocese and retire to a monastery in Cork! Needless to say, no official announcement appeared; but a sheepish note from his lawyers, his sudden departure from Killygobragh, and grapevine news of his present abode, made one super-fluous. It was something the minds of the *Globe* men could barely envisage. They felt as a team might feel, straining every nerve and sinew in a tug of war, were the other side simply to let go. Metaphorically speaking, they lay about on the ground and gasped.

It is not, however, in the nature of newspaper men to lie gasping about on the ground for long. Very soon they were on their legs again, looking for work. It crossed their eager restless minds that the facts of the notorious demo had never been fully explored. Had there been one, or had there not? The authorities involved preserved their secret inviolate. Women's Lib had been roughed up too often by the Press to give it the least cooperation. The whole thing rested on the word of a young reporter who—as the aunt of the *Globe*'s deputy editor was willing to take oath—had been at a party miles away from where the outrage was said to have taken place.

And the topic itself was very much in the air. Half the citizens of the country were hammering away at the media, day after day. From morning to night a bearded youth paced grimly up and down before the Dáil, waving a poster which plugged 'the fundamental right of all human beings to be born.' A platoon of the Children of Mary had picketed a neighbouring hotel, under the impression that this was the Dáil itself, and were driven off by some angry old men with umbrellas. A *Globe* photographer chanced to be leaving the Dáil just as this happened and got a picture which, over the caption *Massacre of the Innocents,* whipped up their public's fury a hundredfold.

The *Globe* accordingly felt the hour had come for a battle unto the death. Bringing up its heavy artillery, it led off with a roar to the effect that there had never been a demo, at any time or in any place. No one, by now, cared in the slightest whether there had been or not. The point at issue was, were you a good Catholic and Irishman, or a sleazy unprincipled long-haired layabout.

All this made Magee of the *Inquirer* a very unhappy man. For one thing, there could no longer be any question of that lawsuit, so lovingly prepared, which was to have pulverized the *Globe* for ever. To go on with it now, would be madness. And then, there was the matter of the article itself. He had believed Dermot's story, still did believe it, had printed it in the leading place; and had then, as he thought, neutralized it by his editorial, condemning the whole escapade. But in the present effervescence of public opinion, this was not enough. The *Globe* faction were howling for Dermot's blood, demanding to know why anyone so devoid of conscience was still in the *Inquirer*'s employ and, even worse, was allowed to cover momentous stories like the founding of the Cistercian apiary at Ballytubber. Magee was not going to throw the boy to the wolves merely because they expressed a desire to tear him limb from limb; but he did think it prudent to keep him out of the public eye awhile, until things should settle down.

He therefore summoned him to his office, asked kindly after his health, gave him a drink from his private bar and a cigarette from his silver box, and announced that for the time being he, Dermot, would take over the Book Page.

"The Book Page!" echoed Dermot, his eyes wide with horror. "Sure, nobody ever reads it!"

Such was the deplorable fact.

"Ah, but they will!" cried Magee. "Wait till you have it in hands, they'll be fighting over it. The first thing in the paper they'll look for, it wouldn't surprise me."

"Then it had better go on page one," Dermot remarked in a caustic tone.

A quip like this, from one who could have been thrown overboard altogether without anyone noticing the splash, was not to the editor's taste. "We'll be keeping you on at your old salary," he said, his voice gentle and kind as ever, but with undercurrents in it that Dermot caught and correctly assessed.

He left the office with feelings akin to despair. That no one did more than glance at the *Inquirer* literary page was only one cause of his anguish. It had always been a butt of his, and the reviewers a favourite target. Apart from the veteran hacks who dealt with books on Ireland, her past, present, saints, heroes, lore, myths and scenery, which continued pouring from the presses in a kind of chronic racial diarrhoea, there was no one competent to make any appraisal of anything. Novels were reviewed by failed novelists —not future, brilliant novelists like Dermot Wyllie but by weary old drunks whose faded and dog-eared manuscripts had been finally thrown into a drawer long years ago. Works of a general nature were apt to be dismissed with a cutting phrase or two: since the reviewer had no grasp of the subject at all, he must pretend to one greater than that of the author himself, or risk looking an ignoramus. And so on, and so on.

There was a certain amount of truth in the aphorisms Dermot scattered about so freely, and which were swiftly passed on to the appropriate ears. But never in his darkest moments had he dreamed of sinking into this underworld himself. It might almost be preferable to patrol the Birdcage Walk or Shepherds Bush with P. C. Maguire. And who would he ever find, even among those down to their last penny, that would contribute to any page of his? There were certain literary editors in Dublin who wrote reviews themselves, signing them with fictitious names that took nobody in: Dermot had always been particularly amusing at their expense, and now he saw the day approach when he must join their squalid ranks himself.

This, then, was one of the woes that lay on his mind

when he met Nuala: another, almost as dire, touched Nuala herself. Quite simply, he did not wish and never really had wished to marry her. They had met when the dislike of her parents, particularly of her mother, normal to her age, was at its zenith. Whatever either of them might say, it was incumbent on her to oppose. As for the convent, all she seemed to have brought away was the memory of boredom by the hour, of polished wood or oilcloth smelling faintly of lavender, of the peculiar rustle of nuns' skirts, of holy pictures everywhere that no one ever looked at, of fits of giggles in class or of sobs in the dormitory, and of the chapel tower with its spiral stairway and rose windows here and there, through which she often gazed longingly at the sea. To say that Dermot seduced her would be inaccurate, for she yielded to his advances with no great reluctance. Her only fear was of being found out. And yet for all that, she was innocence itself. She assumed that this procedure was the up-to-date style of courtship and must end in marriage, just as her parents' years of 'walking out' and timidly holding hands had done.

By a strange coincidence, a few words she let fall brought this home to Dermot at the very moment he was thinking it nearly time to drop her. But some days later, by a coincidence stranger still, and indeed by a dispensation so strange as to border on the marvellous, Brian was appointed Minister of State. Once the initial shock was over, Dermot began to see things in a different light. He was a youth who regarded human beings purely as they affected himself; and if he did not want Nuala as a wife, he was quite reconciled to the Minister as a father-in-law.

And this particular Ministry appeared so solid and safe, being founded on dreams. The bringing home to Ireland of her 'exiles,' who were having the time of Riley where they were and whom nothing would have induced to move, was far up in the realm of fantasy, like the revival of the Irish tongue and the unification of the country; and simply because it was so, a Ministry set up to deal with it could never be abolished. With a change of government Brian might find himself unemployed for a spell; but then his party would get in again and back he would go, by natural right, as the biggest fool in the bag.

So Dermot reasoned, and his reasoning up to a point was sound. But of late he had been seriously doubting if Brian would survive, even in this restful backwater. Since his promotion, he had been more often in St Paddy's than out: what if those stretches of time when his powers were denied to the nation grew longer and longer until they, so to speak, met, and his residence in the Home became perpetual?

Dermot was pondering this hazard when called to the editor's office, where the appalling news he received drove it out of his mind. Now it came back with new force as he sat with Nuala in Davy Byrnes's, listening to her happy excited chatter. Far from sharing her pleasure, he found it the very last straw that she should be raised to eminence just as he had about reached rock bottom. He immediately went to work to try and spoil it for her.

"How's your father?" he struck in abruptly, with Nuala in full spate about Bracken.

"I don't know. I haven't seen him yet." Nuala was hurt and a little angry. "Why the sudden interest in Daddy? You never asked about him before. Have you nothing to say about RTE?"

"What do you expect me to say?"

"You could congratulate me, anyhow."

"On hitching up with that old has-been of a corn merchant? I didn't realize that it was a matter for congratulation."

"You were keen enough on my going in for the commercials."

This was true, but his motives there had been purely economic, the cost of living, cannabis included, having risen sharply again over the summer. The last thing he had in mind was that Nuala should acquire any personal status.

"That was different," he snapped back. "The money was good and nobody saw you. You'll make a right Judy of yourself, churning out the old stuff week after week. One of these homing emigrants, I'll bet, renouncing all to be near her old Mammy, who's not too well just now. 'How is it, alanna, back on the old sod?' " he fluted. " 'Ah, bejasus, couldn't I just kneel down and kiss the dear ground itself!' "

Nuala frowned at this all too accurate prognosis. "Isn't it a strange thing," she said icily, "that people who do nothing themselves could, if they only liked to bother, do so much more than the ones that actually get there?"

"And what d'you mean by that?"

"Anything you like to find in it."

Dermot was about to let fly in earnest when he remembered the reason for making this rendezvous; and calming himself, he rested his hand on her knee in lover-like fashion and looked at her with gentle pathos. "Don't mind me, I'm rather worried just now," he said. "Something awkward happened me. I wonder now, could you let me have £25?"

"And what do you want it for?"

"Well . . . it sounds pretty queer." Anytime Dermot spoke the truth, it had a way of sounding queer: he had often been struck by this fact. "Do you remember that day in the Green, when that dog ran off with my pants? Well, God alone knows where they got to, but I'm being blackmailed."

"Blackmailed? because Rusty ran off with your pants?"

"Because of what was in them. Wait now." Dermot fished in his pocket and brought out a plain brown envelope, such as tradesmen use, containing a message typed by unskilled hands.

"i am in p0ssession of a pair of blu jean pants the p roperty of yourse*f," it said. "THey were pased for scruttiny to me, as a Forensic Analyst, by an official dept.% InvestigatioO revealed severa l GRAins of cannabis in 1 of the pokets. If you will place twentyfive used poun noats in a envelope, put this between the page ss of a newspaper, drop same in the literbin beside the Bonk of Ireland at 3.30 pM exactly tomorrow and walk straight down Dame Street without *looking Back* you will hear no more. I give you my word of honour, the pants will be drooped in the Liffey the minyute after I collect."

The signature was notable too, as it ran: ~~GERALD DODDER~~ Your Well-wisher. Finally, there was a postscript: "I wouddnnt have wished this, only I need the money."

Nothing is so baffling to the Irish mind as a simple direct statement that means what it says, just that and no more. The writer of this communication was a forensic analyst, was in possession of the pants, had been requested to examine them, had found the cannabis. He only departed from the truth in his reference to an official department: the task had in fact been entrusted to him by the deputy editor of the *Globe,* who had jealously hoarded the pants in the office safe until Mr Dodder's return from holiday. All else was authentic, down to his signature, which on second thoughts he had decided not to reveal, and to the point of his needing some money.

Nevertheless, clear and straightforward as it was, it threw both Dermot and Nuala into a turmoil of speculation. They cudgelled their brains, trying to elucidate its real meaning and guess what lay behind it: to imagine how Rusty had come to place the garment in official hands and how it had been identified. They shivered to think to what Wagnerian excesses the whole affair was but a prelude—

what if a posse of Guards rushed forward to seize Dermot just as he was dropping the precious bundle in the bin? Their mystification grew on consulting the telephone book and finding the name Dodder, Gerald Aloysius, followed by the initials M.I.Ph.C. But argue to and fro as they would they always ended up at the same conclusion: whatever the consequences, they had no choice but to comply with the instructions as they stood.

"So can you let me have the money?" Dermot said, in his sweetest voice.

"I suppose I will have to," Nuala replied, with reluctance. "But I hope to God the fellow is honest."

On the following day she drew the sum from her bank and gave it to Dermot, who sealed it in an envelope and rolled a copy of the *Globe* round it. At the last moment, the braver of the two, she proposed hovering near the litterbin herself until their tormentor collected his ransom, when she would confront him, demanding its return and the pants as well; but Dermot would not hear of it.

"I mightn't be as lucky as you were yesterday," he said, referring to the procedures in the District Court. "If anything went wrong now, I could go inside."

He dropped the paper in the bin and, with heavy hearts, they walked off together down Dame Street without looking back, as Mr Dodder had directed. They might have found a crumb of comfort in the sequel: for Mr Dodder, than whom no one had ever been more felicitously named, was musing on some chemical problem at the time and, having collected the swag, absently dropped it in the river and the pants as well. He was a man of principle, however, and grievous as the discovery was when he made it, he still held to his bargain.

"I examined that garment you gave me," he told Eamon Kelly, who was almost breathless with excitement. "Nothing there at all."

"Nothing?"

"No."

"Where are they now?" barked Eamon. "I should like a second opinion."

"I am afraid the chemicals we have to use destroyed the fabric. My fee is £25," he added, hanging up before a discussion could develop.

That day's issue of the *Globe* carried, in a box with Dermot's photograph—a smirking one taken shortly after his famous scoop—a carefully phrased congratulation to him on his new appointment, "a post we have always believed well suited to him and to which, we understand, he himself has always aspired": every word of which, as Eamon intended, was another thorn in his riven, bleeding heart.

He could not bear this reptile-house of a city much longer. And yet, where else could he go? And wouldn't they all be laughing at him if he ran away? No, he must face it out. Some time his luck would turn, and he'd be the one to laugh. But at this particular moment, he could have sat down and cried like a baby.

fourteen

Grainne's life was such that many times she had the feeling of one who tosses up and down in a frail boat through a heavy sea. Brian came home from his cure, fit and well, apparently a man renewed; and she was poised on the tip of a wave. Then there was the business of the summons and Brian's outbreak, and she slid down into a trough so deep, there hardly could be any hope of rising again. Yet rise she did, that same night, as Nuala came in, so radiant and transformed; but it was only to plunge steeply with the episode of the burning whisky, the fracas with Geraldine and the broadside from Lady Belling.

At the present she was fairly scorching along, like a

speedboat that bounds over the water rather than cuts through it, thanks to the outcome of Nuala's case in District Court No 8. Concerning this, she had no precise information, since nothing appeared in the papers, nor did she want any. She only knew her little lamb was innocent, that the whole affair had been somebody's blunder and was now put right. In consequence, Brian pulled himself together and, his portfolio stuffed with comics, was daily and ceremoniously conveyed to the Ministry or the Dáil. Surely calm water was reached at last, and there must be plain sailing henceforward? She looked on to a happy autumn of gracious living and elegant entertainment, as befitted the wife of a man of national importance.

The first thing to be done was to put herself in trim. What with the holidays and the various upheavals, she had neglected her appearance all summer. Now she went to the fashionable place in Grafton Street where 'everyone' went, and endured a full facial treatment, wax, deep cleanse and massage.

"Try not to smile," the assistant reproved her, spreading the hot wax on her upper lip and chin.

Grainne had suddenly thought of Sister Dolours's own luxuriant growth and her conviction that it was somehow pleasing to the eyes of the Lord.

"Ouch!" she yelled as the wax was ripped of.

"All over now, and you're smooth as an egg."

At the very end the young woman gave her an exciting new make-up—everything had to be 'exciting' this year— with a pearly eye-shadow and bronze lipstick, before passing her on to the hairdresser, who gave her an exciting new cut and, discovering 'a few grey hairs' as she discreetly put it, an exciting copper rinse. Meanwhile, the manicurist busied herself lending a touch of excitement to her neglected fingernails.

"I shouldn't be doing all this," she said, smiling complacently at her reflection in the looking-glass. "An old woman like me!"

"Old woman indeed! Go 'way out of that!" said the hairdresser, as she invariably did, twenty times a day if once.

As Grainne emerged, resplendent, from her cubicle, a hand was laid in easy familiar fashion on her arm. It must be, her guardian angel had fixed the appointment this afternoon for, turning, she found herself face to face with Mrs de Smythe, the President's wife; and Mrs de Smythe was smiling most graciously.

"It's been too long since I saw you, Grainne," she said. "Well, there were the holidays. Had you a great time?"

"Oh, great, simply great," Grainne replied effusively, her tribulations forgotten at once in the glory of this encounter. Everyone was stopping work to watch the informal chat between herself and the First Lady of the Land.

"They tell me Nuala was lovely on television the other night," Mrs de Smythe went on in her regal manner, which she tried to model on that of Queen Elizabeth, with but partial success. "I missed it—Turkish ambassador dining— but I'll be sure to see the next instalment. How nice for you and Brian to have such a brilliant daughter!" And with another little friendly pat on Grainne's arm she moved away, evenly distributing smiles all round.

Grainne left the establishment treading on air. Recognition, Christian names, compliments, the President's wife and perhaps the President as well among Nuala's admiring viewers! Well, and why not? The Hoolahans, after all, belonged to the upper crust these days: it was absurd, having to remind herself of the fact so often.

But as time went on, she grew conscious of something in people's manner to her which she could never define or pin down, but which made her somehow uneasy. As no one made any explicit remarks, it was impossible even to guess what was in their minds; but they had a way of looking and smiling and catching each other's eye that seemed to have a positive malevolence behind it. Gradually she realized that somehow or other it was connected with Nuala, and thought that it must be envy. Not one of her friends had a child that had ever distinguished itself, and her daughter's meteoric rise must have caused resentment. She told herself that it was simply fallen human nature, and remembered them in her prayers.

Then one morning her suspicions were turned in a new and awful direction. She had gone into Beauchamps' to lay in some of the sweets that Brian always clamoured for when deprived of alcohol, and saw Julia Hogan, Peggy O'Rourke and a Dr Rose Slattery at one of the tables, making a hearty meal of cream buns and chocolate éclairs. Quickly, she looked away and made for the counter, but it was too late. All three women knew they were seen and that she wished to ignore them, and all promptly took offence.

"Come and join us, Grainne!" Peggy sang out. "Or are you too grand altogether?"

There was no help for it after that. "I'll just take a coffee," Grainne said, sitting down, resigned. "There's no end to do this morning."

"We were just talking about Petra Slieve," said Dr Slattery, a woman Grainne hardly knew but much disliked.

"Oh?" she said.

It seemed that Petra had carried her economic theories too far and was serving a month in gaol.

"And from the Bambino Gesú!" remarked Julia. "A wild lot of girls they seem to collect these days."

"Ah now, Julia," Grainne remonstrated mildly. "Petra's only one."

The women exchanged little glances and smiled cosily at their buns. At another table near by, Grainne observed, those two vultures Doreen Lehane and Eva Kelly were straining their ears to catch what was said.

"Well? Do you know of any others?"

"No, no, *no!*" replied Julia, as if to say, Perish the thought!

But Grainne felt vaguely disquieted all the same.

"And how's Nuala?" asked Peggy, in the bright tone of one who introduces a fresh and unrelated topic. "Does she often get to Belfast these days?"

"Indeed she does not, why would she? I never knew why she went there at all."

"We all thought, it must be she was on some secret mission," Peggy said innocently.

More glances followed this remark, and Dr Slattery put a hand over her mouth in none too elegant a fashion. Now Eva Kelly wagged her head from side to side, as a bird does when sharpening its beak.

"Ah, the mothers, it's us the poor creatures," Julia sighed. "What do our children ever tell us? The whole of Dublin could be talking them over, and we'd be the last ones to hear of it."

"Do you mean, Nuala is getting herself talked over?" demanded Grainne, her colour rising.

"Not at all, Grainne. You're too quick altogether."

"What do you mean, then? You must mean something."

"I was speaking in a general sort of way. Mrs Slieve never knew Petra was in trouble till she read it in the paper."

"I'm for another cream horn," Peggy declared, changing her voice again as before. "I shouldn't take it, but I will. Forbidden fruit was always the sweetest. Dr Macnamara says I'll kill myself yet."

Here Dr Slattery burst into a ringing laugh that made everyone in the café look round.

"Excuse me, I couldn't help it," she spluttered. "It was

thinking of Eoghen Macnamara. Did you hear the latest? He got out an affidavit that a certain accused person was unfit to appear in Court, and took it there himself in case they wanted his evidence."

"And wasn't it like him?" asked Peggy. It was clear that she knew the story and was feeding lines to the narrator, like a stooge. "Oh, he's the decentest man that ever trod leather! Nothing to laugh at in that, I'm sure."

"Yes, but the accused person was there before him and had already been dealt with," Dr Slattery proceeded, choking again. "And Mac had deposed that sh . . . that the individual was in bed, under heavy sedation! I don't know how he gets away with it, I know I never could."

"Ah, he'll only say it was against his advice and without his knowledge."

Grainne finished her coffee in a daze and left as soon as she could. So that was it! The story had leaked out, and all Dublin was chortling over it. But the child was innocent, the case was dismissed, there wasn't a spot on her name. And yet those three witches appeared to know more about it than she did, and so did the eavesdroppers at the table beyond. The whole lot had been revelling in some information denied to her, the only one with a right to know. As she drove homeward, she attempted to calm her mind by repeating the Loreto, a practice of hers in time of trouble . . . *Mother most amiable, Mother most admirable, Mother of good Counsel, Mother of our Creator, Mother of our Saviour, Virgin most prudent* . . . At this point, for some odd psychological reason, she stuck fast. *Virgin most prudent, Virgin most prudent,* what came after *Virgin most prudent*? Her mind went completely blank. *Virgin most prudent* . . . No. And what was so prudent about Her at all? She had repeated the words thousands of times without ever stopping to think what they meant. God help her, this was blasphemy.

Holy Mother of God, come to my aid. Now it crossed her mind that she had promised, if Nuala came through unscathed, to do the pilgrimage to Knock. She had not done so, and Knock would shortly close for the winter. But was Nuala unscathed? Was she even innocent? Belfast. Belfast. Belfast. Ah, but she couldn't, she never would. Young people said things to shock their parents, but they were sound. Were they not. *Virgin most prudent . . .* No, she could not get past it, her mind stayed boggling there like Balaam's ass.

"Holy Mary, give me a sign," she prayed with all her heart, "and I'll go to Knock." But a sign there must be, she was not going all that way without one. She had been taken in before. Dear Heaven, what was she thinking now? More blasphemy. It must be the Devil was at her, or she was tainted by the company she had just been keeping. Well, this should be a lesson to her. From now on she would pass them by, and associate exclusively with her peers.

fifteen

It was only natural that Nuala's good fortune should make her a number of enemies. Some of them were merely jealous of her beauty, or of the effortless way she had launched herself, or of the fact that she became a celebrity almost overnight. Others disapproved of her on moral grounds—for by now her story had slowly wended its way round the city—or would have rejoiced to think of her washing clothes in some penitential convent. And it had all happened so fast, she had had no time to learn the airs of assumed modesty that make the famous tolerable. Apart from this, Dublin is ever inclined to look coldly on the successful. Dr Johnson was mistaken when he declared that the Irish never speak well of each other. They crack up their own more eloquently than any other people on earth, but for this to happen there are three indispensable qualifications: the subject of their eulogies has to be ruined, convicted of some disgraceful crime, or dead.

Less natural, however, was the fact that no one was more jealous, more hostile and more scathing than her own true love. Indeed, the reversal of their rôles was too much for him to stomach. He felt it like a physical pain in his chest, as if he had too hastily swallowed a doughnut. It was as if a contract between them as to their relative status had been shamelessly and cynically broken. He lost his sleep, his manhood ebbed away, and the books on his page were ground so small, it became a matter of comment among even the crocodiles of the Dublin literary world.

In this last respect, sooner or later things were bound to come to a head. The authors had for some time manifested their dissatisfaction in various ways, from vituperation to physical assault, but now a more redoubtable figure entered the fray. Returning from lunch one afternoon, Dermot found a note on his desk to the effect that the editor wished to see him at once.

Magee had before him a volume just out, entitled *Eamon de Valera: a New Appraisal,* and a proof of Dermot's own review, ripping the book to pieces and headed 'That Old Druid Again.' There was no drink or cigarette today, not even the offer of a chair: Magee's bushy brows were in a straight line across his forehead and ferocity lurked in his eyes: all in all, at that moment, he resembled a mandril more than a human being.

"Who is Bernard de Montmorency?" he demanded, this being the latest nom-de-plume that Dermot had bestowed upon himself.

"A young chap I thought deserved trying out," Dermot

replied, in what he hoped was an offhand manner, although it was clear that an explosion was on the way.

"Since when do important books go out to deserving young chaps?" Magee inquired, frowning more horribly still. Then he added in his grimmest tone, "Deserving young chaps with fanciful and improbable names?"

"I don't think I understand you, sir . . ."

"Oh? Get me this Montmorency on the phone, will you?"

"He hasn't one, sir," Dermot stammered. "I have to leave messages for him at Mooney's Lounge."

Magee leaned back in his chair and folded his arms. "I imagine you know that we have a proprietor," he said with heavy sarcasm. "You may not, however, be aware that Dr McEvoy, the author of this book, is the proprietor's brother-in-law. He also belongs to the Institute of Advanced Studies, as is clearly shown on the jacket. Furthermore, Eamon de Valera is one of the greatest Irishmen that ever lived and readers of the *Inquirer* will not expect to see him referred to as 'that old Druid.' " Here he paused, to light a cigar and puff the smoke towards Dermot, as always when in a dangerous mood.

"I'm very sorry indeed, sir. I ought to have sent the book to someone with greater experience."

Magee removed the cigar from his mouth, examined the tip, replaced it and puffed vigorously for some moments in silence. Then he took it out again and said, "There is no such person as Bernard de Montmorency. You wrote this tripe yourself, without even a glance at the blurb, and you added that offensive heading."

This wholly accurate statement had the effect, as accurate statements in Dublin are wont to do, of making the person involved so angry that he lost all sense of fear.

"Do you doubt my word, Mr Magee?"

"I certainly do."

"Then I resign," said Dermot, drawing himself up.

"No, you don't. You're fired. Accounts have your cheque ready. Collect and leave at once."

"First you demote me, from sheer lack of integrity and moral cowardice," Dermot cried, his voice throbbing with passion. "Now you add insult to injury, and impugn my honour. But my God, you hoor, you've not heard the last of this!" And he flung out of the room, slamming the door as he went, leaving Magee to sit there, puffing faster and ever faster.

This exchange of views took place at roughly three o'clock. Dermot spent the afternoon lying on his bed at home and glaring at the ceiling. The Angelus had long since rung before he could even start to plan his moves, his brain was in such a turmoil. What he would really have liked, would be to blow the newspaper offices up; but lacking the equipment and experience for operations of that sort, he determined instead to write Magee a letter that would make him writhe with shame and remorse and wring from him complete satisfaction.

He wrote, as usual, like Shakespeare, never blotting out a line, and freely borrowing from that poet to lend force and elegance to his rebuke.

Sir,
Who steals my purse, steals trash; 'tis something, nothing;
'Twas mine, 'tis his, and has been slave to thousands;
But he that filches from me my good name
Robs me of that which not enriches him,
And makes me poor indeed.

These great words from the greatest of English poets may or may not be familiar to you, but they apply in every way to your treatment of myself. True, you never repudiated my story of the demo in so many words, but by your actions you did. Your reducing me to the Book Page, than which only the Women's Section or the Gardening Notes could have degraded me further, notified Dublin, Ireland and the world of your lack of confidence in my integrity. Such was my reward for coming up with the first real story in any national paper for months and months.

And did your persecution stop at that? No. You inquire as to the authorship of a review that I, misguidedly perhaps but in all good faith, had commissioned and when I answer you promptly and candidly, you tell me to my face that I am a liar and that I wrote the piece myself.

I have borne much in the past weeks but this goes beyond the limits of human endurance. I propose to begin a hunger-strike forthwith and shall continue it until you

1) Apologize to me fully, and in writing

2) Reinstate me in my former and rightful position

3) Raise my salary by £200 a year

4) Undertake that no similiar affronts shall ever be offered again.

Should you refuse these reasonable conditions, my blood will be on your head, as I shall continue fasting even unto death. For what is life without honour? To such a man as I, nothing, less than nothing.

Having dashed this off and signed his name with a flourish, he considered adding a postscript, 'Bernard de Montmorency wishes to associate himself with all that pertains to the review,' this character having by now, as it were, sprung to life and being entitled to put in a word; but he decided against it, as a possible complication. He sealed the letter up, hurried out to post it and returned home, complacently assured of bringing Magee to his senses; and settled down to a hearty meal.

"Answer him for me, like a good man," Magee said to

his deputy, throwing the missive across the table when he had finished laughing.

"What'll I say?" Seumas asked, when he had also had his laugh out.

"Anything you like."

"Dear Dermot," Seumas wrote, "don't be a bloody eejit. You know the Editor—he'll cool off by and by and then he'll surely do something for you. But it won't be here. We both believe you might do well in publicity, think about it. Yours, Seumas Duff."

In a general way, no one was shrewder than Dermot in sizing things up or predicting their outcome. Tell him that so-and-so was bringing a lawsuit, for example, and he would reveal that the action would never come on, as the party was merely fooling about. Tell him an investigation into some political scandal was pending and he would, correctly, forecast the result or deny it would ever be held. Tell him that someone was starting up in business, and he apparently knew by instinct if the man would succeed or fail. He was not, of course, infallible. In assuring Nuala she would hear no more of the business at Connolly station, he had reckoned without the bulldog strain in Ruairí na Rigg. When, to cover his slip over the baby giraffe, he blurted out the story of the demo to Magee, the last thing he anticipated the prudish fellow would do was splash it over the front page. But failures of this kind were due to individual quirks there could be no accounting for; and take him all in all, his grasp of situations was remarkable in one so young.

This enviable gift, however, deserted him at once if the situation happened to involve himself. If some friend had written that letter to Magee and asked his opinion of it, he would have laughed uproariously and urged him to tear it up. But, composed by himself, he had every faith in it. Even if his demands were not met in full by return of post, he was confident of receiving a telephone call to hurry round and talk things over. The brief mocking reply of Seumas Duff amazed and flabbergasted him, and filled him with horror at man's cruelty to man.

It posed as well the thorny problem of what to do next. Was he, as he had threatened, to go on hunger-strike? It was the fashionable thing just now, but those who did so were all in the public eye. What was the point of starving to death at home, and Magee not a penny the wiser? and with Nuala popping in and out and telling him not to be silly? Not that she popped in so often these days, in fact she was decidedly cool. Women were irrational, unstable creatures altogther. She had always taken such pride in the idea that he was an artist, a creator, a being that stood above the common run of men; and now, because he was true to that divine calling, would not betray that spark of the godhead in him, but applied to her work such well-judged terms as 'piffle' or 'crap,' she had turned against him.

She would be playing now this minute, he remembered, and moodily switched his television on. There she was, cradling a lamb in her arms with her cheek pressed to its woolly face, and talking over a fence to the handsome young farmer who was clearly billed to marry her. "Isn't he the little doat?" she was cooing, in a frightful stagey brogue. "Ah, he does well enough for just now," the farmer cooed back, in a patois equally loathsome: "but the day'll come when 'tis a gossoon ye'll be fondling there, and maybe not so long off either!"

"Jesus bloody Christ!" Dermot switched off in a fury and threw himself on the bed.

His street bell rang, adding to his annoyances. Let it. He was not going down three flights of stairs for what was probably nothing important. Then it rang again, insistently, and he could hear some officious person from another flat going to see who was there. Heavy steps came up the stairway, and a heavy hand pounded on his door; a stern voice said, "Open up now, will you? We know you're inside."

The callers were two uniformed Gardai, armed with a search warrant and looking for cannabis, which they sniffed out of its hiding-place with the singleminded devotion of pigs on a truffle-hunt.

"Honest to God, I never knew it was there," Dermot pleaded, as they took out their notebooks. "Must have been left behind by the lad who rented the place before."

"Go 'way out of that," was the unfeeling reply.

The Drug Squad had just completed a thoroughgoing study of the life, habits, premises and personal memoranda of Mr Abdul Hamid with whom, in what seemed to be no time at all, Dermot found himself sharing a Black Maria to the Bridewell. Now and then it would pause to take up a new customer, and all were to appear on the following day before Justice Magadoo, who was back at work, quite coherent, and who took a most serious view of drug offences.

"You owe me twenty pounds," Abdul Hamid muttered, as the car rattled along beside the Liffey. He was a plump oily Tangerine, with exclusively commercial ideas.

"In me eye!" Dermot muttered back. "Ten, more like it."

"By the time we get out, that will be worth no more than five. Therefore you owe me twenty." Mr Hamid's reasoning invariably ran along these lines.

"Well, it doesn't signify, as I have no money at all."

"Then who's to pay my lawyer?"

"Shut your gobs, there," said a Guard.

For supper that night there were lumps of fried black pudding adrift in a bowl of glaucous soup, which looked as nasty as it smelled. Dermot picked up a spoon, but laid it down with a shiver as a cheerful cockney voice beside him said: " 'Ere goes for a swim in the Mediterrighnean."

"Eat up, you," a warder instructed Dermot. "We haven't all night."

It was now, with things apparently at their lowest ebb, that Dermot had one of his finest inspirations. "Not me," he said. "I'm on hunger-strike."

"Want us to tempt you with orange juice and brandy, eh?" the warder quipped. "Well, better think again."

Dermot leaned back and folded his arms. Other officials were called but nothing would induce the prisoner to touch the soup or, next morning, the equally repulsive repast that was served. As he had eaten nothing at all since Seumas Duff's note had arrived to wreck his peace of mind on the previous day, by the time he stood in the dock he did present a worn and haggard appearance; and, on being asked how he wished to plead, merely shook his head and swayed to and fro, as one about to faint.

"This would seem to be a very bad case," Justice Magadoo observed, smacking his lips after the prosecutor had opened and the police had had their say. "Who's defending?"

"No one, your Worship," replied the prosecutor, Mr Burke. "The prisoner declines to be represented. And I gather he is on hunger-strike."

"Hunger-strike!" echoed the Justice, sharply. "We don't want any of that nonsense here. Not political, is he?"

"Not as far as we know, your Worship."

"Well then, he's come to the wrong shop. What have you to say about it, Wyllie?"

"I am fasting, unto death if need be," Dermot said faintly, with a sidelong glance at the Press, all busy writing. "To clear my reputation. I have been traduced, reviled and hounded from my job, simply because I, and I alone, dared to write the truth. And,

> "Who steals my purse, steals trash; 'tis something, nothing;
> 'Twas mine, 'tis his, and has been slave to thousands;
> But he that filches from me my good name
> Robs me of that which not enriches him,
> And makes me poor indeed . . ."

"You certainly have the gift of the gab," the Justice broke in, not without a certain unwilling admiration. "But where is all this guff bringing us? What's this about hounding and reviling and truth? We're talking about cannabis."

"I refer your Worship to my disclosure of the Women's Lib demo at Connolly last summer, which no other journalist dared to print and which the authorities hushed up. And now my own paper has gone back on me. I am unemployed, penniless, and with nothing but the knowledge of my innocence to sustain me," said Dermot, the tears starting to his eyes.

"Are we never to hear the last of that demo?" the Justice barked. "Especially as there wasn't one. Keep to the point at issue, prisoner, or you will do yourself no good. The Gardai found cannabis on your premises, and you have all the looks of the kind who take it."

"Looks, your Worship, looks!" said Dermot, with a gentle compassion for such naiveté. "What are looks to go by? An ignorant man could say, from *your* looks, that you were the kind who took a drop too many. And what a fistful of fools that man would be!"

There were praiseworthy but unsuccessful attempts to hold back the mirth which greeted this sally from all sides of the room.

Magadoo's complexion, always the colour of a ripe pippin, darkened to a shade not far from that of a blackberry. "Is this fellow right in the head?" he demanded, glaring at Dermot over his spectacles. "I don't believe he is. The case is held over, till a medical report is to hand."

The period that followed was in nearly all respects a happy and fruitful one for Dermot. For some days the pangs of appetite were fierce, but then they passed, leaving only a pleasant languor. The prison doctor who was to make the report was young, in favour of birth control, possessed of the truth about the demo and wholly on Dermot's side. "At last, a man of principle!" he exclaimed. "It's what the country badly needs." He said, therefore, that he wished to keep Dermot under close observation and had him moved to the hospital, where he was given a room to himself and several pretty nurses. Nobody, not even the chaplain, sought to dissuade him from the hunger-strike, this being at the moment one of Ireland's sacred cows.

He lay comfortably in bed, re-living the scene in Court, his impassioned outburst, his saucy rejoinder to Justice Magadoo, and wondering how it all had looked in the papers, and what kind of bulletins were printed about his condition from day to day. This was his only grief: nothing was said as to newspapers—no doubt the authorities feared to excite or tire him—and he was too proud to ask. Heroes do not inquire how they stand in the world's opinion: it must suffice merely to lie there, revelling in the thought of it.

But time passed and there was no word from Magee, of remorse, anxiety or anything else. His long abstinence began to make itself felt in new and disagreeable ways. There were fainting fits and dizzy spells and frightening hallucinations. He no longer needed to stage his effects for the nurses, lying back on the pillows with eyes closed, hands plucking feebly at the coverlet: all were genuine.

At last the terrible truth came home, that they were actually going to let him die. There was nothing in the world he could do to stop them. Those who starved themselves to death were objects of veneration; but those who gave up, even at the eleventh hour, were figures of fun and could never hold up their heads again. Death was better than shame or, rather, ridicule. And he was now too weak even to glory in the prospect of his funeral, the nationwide mourning that would follow and the assurance of a place in history.

He was lying, numb and torpid, when he became aware of a rough male voice addressing him, it seemed from a long way off, and a gentle female one expostulating with it.

"Now what tomfoolery is this?" the voice was demanding. "You're a perfect little pest and always have been."

"Oh, Professor Wyllie," the nurse softly reproached him. "Please don't distress my patient. He's very low."

"I can see that," was the brusque reply. "Who authorized all this? What's the meaning of it?"

"Don't you read the papers, Father?" Dermot whispered.

"Papers! The printers have all been on strike since October 6. And the radio and TV men as well."

October the sixth was the day of Dermot's magnificent performance in Court. The shock was so great that he made an effort to sit up in bed. "Do you mean, there's been nothing published about me?" he croaked.

"Of course there hasn't. I was at a conference in Geneva and when I come back, it is to find out purely by chance that you've been arrested for drugging, that the Justice has called for a report on your mental condition—which doesn't surprise me—and that you're throwing a hunger-strike. Now, nurse, be good enough to take immediate steps to feed this boy."

The nurse bridled. "I take my instructions from Dr Synge . . ."

"Oh dear me no, you don't. Kindly do as I say. I'll be having a word or two with this Dr Synge, and with some others. And as soon as this young ass is well enough, I'm having him moved to my own hospital." His voice suddenly changed, becoming quiet, pensive and profoundly lugubrious. "I really believe, this whole bloody country is insane."

In such a manner, ingloriously, terminated the martyrdom of Dermot Wyllie. On the whole, however, it seemed to him that things might have been worse. He was not really, when it came to the point, the stuff of which martyrs were made; and if the world were not even to hear about him, there was no sense in it whatsoever.

síxteen

It was shortly after the events described above that Brian, as Minister for Social Adjustment, made his tremendous speech in the Dáil. This speech was entirely spontaneous and unpremeditated. No one had tabled a motion requiring a reply, nor had he given notice of any intention to address the assembly. As, relatively though not completely sober, he took his seat, no such purpose was in his mind. In fact, he felt somewhat drowsy and rested there for twenty minutes or so, hardly aware of what was going on. But then, of a sudden, it was as if a Power outside himself, beyond him and higher, took possession and jerked him to his feet, to plead a cause with a moving eloquence he had never known was his.

It struck him also that the beautifully proportioned room, a heritage from the alien oppressor, was packed as never before. Not only were all the deputies present but the public gallery, behind those glass walls that occasionally put the frivolous in mind of a Zoo, was crowded as well. The Press were there to a man, Ring-sider scribbling away at top speed. Even the Speaker, bewigged and gowned in his chair, who as a rule sat through speeches with a kind of somnolent resignation, had his chin thoughtfully cupped in his hand. For Brian treated of matters close to every Irish heart.

It was the strained attention, the murmurs of approval, the occasional little bursts of applause, that brought home to him the extent of his triumph. He himself was so carried away that he hardly knew what he said. His subject was, the Irish in exile, thousands, nay millions, forced by cruel circumstances (which could be traced back to the Famine and Queen Victoria's Government) to live far from home.

That they were an asset to the country that housed them, that they were as a leaven there, a quickening, enriching, enlivening element, was a fact that admitted of no denial. But what of themselves? What of their hunger, their pain, their longing for the beautiful land of their birth? What of the empty homesteads, those dear white cabins, where first they saw the light of day and, somewhat later, lisped their first little prayers? We saw, did we not, in the great foreign cities, New York, Boston, Cleveland, London, Manchester, Liverpool, how heroically they strove to keep the great old traditions alive. We saw them too, with a noble sacrifice of money, of liberty, yes, of life itself, associate themselves with Ireland's glorious struggle for freedom and unity. We saw them strike down our enemies, denounce the myrmidons of tyranny and destroy their seats of power and their collections of wealth. More than once we saw them marching fearless through the hostile streets of British imperialism, shouting defiance at it, proudly dressed in the proscribed republican uniform, the tricolour waving aloft, and nothing between them and the fury of a soulless mob but a handful of English bobbies. We saw them and bowed down before them in gratitude and pride.

But were pride and gratitude enough? A thousand times, No. Ireland must transform herself, must work her fingers to the bone to create a country able to receive them back, to create living conditions equal or superior to those they had enjoyed elsewhere. To this one aim, all his energies were at the present time directed. He had this very week requested the Archbishop of Dublin—and His Grace had consented with delight—to proclaim a National Day of the Exile, when masses for the well-being and swift return of Ireland's sons and daughters would be said in every Catholic church throughout the length and breadth of the Republic. For, without the help of Almighty God, we could do nothing . . .

Such were the inspiring words, or others very like them, that tripped off Brian's tongue, in a mellifluous tenor far removed from his usual husky croak. But when he got to the Almighty, a most extraordinary thing occurred. All at once, he discovered, he was no longer on his legs, holding the chamber spellbound, but slumped in his chair with someone vigorously pulling his arm; and, opening his bewildered eyes, he identified the assailant as his old enemy Ruairí na Rigg.

"Wake up, Brian, for God's sake," came in the clipped English accent. "You're snoring like a Diesel engine, and Denis Molloy has a question for you."

"You interrupted my speech," Brian growled, rising to his feet with every intention of resuming it.

"Ah, the Minister has finished his little nap," came from Denis Molloy, an assiduous Hoolahan baiter. "I will repeat my question to him. How many people are employed at his Ministry, and what do they do all day?"

"Mr Molloy, if you please," said the Speaker. "I have already ruled that question out of order."

"Well, at a guess, how many? And what do they do all day?"

"Mr Molloy, the answer to the first part of your question is available elsewhere, as you know," the Speaker rebuked him. "The second could, if you so desire, be referred to Oif-ig Aire na Seirbhísí Poiblí."

"Apart from sneaking out for quick ones, reading the comics and waiting for football and racing results?" went on the tenacious Molloy.

"You are not helping the Chair, Mr Molloy," said the Speaker bitterly.

"You got all of that from some bloody spy," snapped the Minister, now fully awake.

"Aha! You admit it!" crowed Mr Molloy, automatically throwing a glance at the Press benches; but the strike was still in progress and these were all but empty.

"Any of you lot I find knocking around, I'll have them thrown out the door," the Minister declared, in a trenchant manner.

"Order, order!" cried the Speaker, feverishly ringing his bell. "Next question. Mr Ryan."

"Will the Minister say . . ." Mr Ryan commenced.

"Your whole set-up's a bloody cod! you'd say the country was made of money. How many exiles did you bring home yet? Tell us that much."

"Mr Molloy will sit down," said the Speaker. Ting-a-ling! Ting-a-ling! "Mr Ryan."

"Will the Minister inform me . . ." Mr Ryan patiently recommenced.

"It's not our department, bringing the exiles home. We are there to help them adjust when they come."

"And when'll that be?"

"Sit down this minute, Mr Molloy, or I shall suspend you." The bell rang again. "Mr Ryan."

"I've forgotten me question," Mr Ryan admitted.

"You better ask Tionscal agus Tráchtáil, or Talmhaíocht," snarled the Minister to Mr Molloy. "I've enough of your feckin' persecution."

"The Minister will withdraw that last observation," the Speaker all but screamed. "This is an utter disgrace."

"I'll do no such a thing," the Minister shouted. "That chancer there is at me morning, noon and night."

"Sure, it's not that often we see you here . . ."

"I work as hard as any feckin' American executive . . ."

"The Minister is suspended! Mr Molloy is supended!" the Speaker all but howled, ringing his bell like one demented.

"We have to take our chance when we can get it," Mr Molloy proceeded, bent on having the final word. "We can't go trapesing off to St Paddy's all the time."

This was the last straw and the Speaker sprang to his feet. "The Chamber will rise. The session is over," he bawled, on the brink of tears. "The Minister and Mr Molloy will both apologize before taking their seats again. Let that be understood."

The Clerk made a note.

"Worse than chimpanzees, a thousand times worse," groaned the Speaker under his breath, as he tore off his wig and left the room with all the speed he could muster. He was not feeling too well that day, having a pain in a tooth: in fact, the proceedings were more or less as they usually were.

The Minister stumbled away to the bar, bemused, at a loss to know what exactly had happened. In later days, recounting the experience, his speech was the part he dwelt on.

seventeen

Strikes in Ireland have the elfin inconsistency of much else in that country. Some drag on for months and months, with a threat of running into years: others collapse in a matter of weeks or days. It is worth noting perhaps that the flimsier the pretext for striking at all, the longer the strike continues. It may be that the Irish find imaginary grievances harder to bear than real ones; but whatever the cause, the industrial action chart is one of caprice and confusion.

The printers' strike was typical in this way. Never had workers so strong a case. Their grumbles about their pay and conditions, which so alarmed the editors, were purely automatic, a matter of form; but censure, or even criticism, they could not abide. When O'Grady of the *Globe* ventured to rebuke the compositor for changing the Bishop's 'to' into 'of,' they were up in arms to a man and indignation meetings were held all over Dublin; and when he followed that up with an objection to 'pubic' instead of 'public,' fury spread all over the land. But what finally put the lid on and brought the presses grinding to a halt was a memorandum from Magee of the *Inquirer,* requesting all compositors to stick by the copy and not to use spelling and punctuation of their own. They were to be robots, it seemed: it was the thin end of the wedge before Fascism took over: their blood boiled and they walked out.

And yet, after only twenty-one days, they walked in again, no one ever knew why. There were no demands for higher wages or shorter hours, or any stipulations of that kind: their one request was that henceforth they should be considered as human beings and not as 'automatoes.'

Without the least idea as to what this petition could mean, the managements gladly assented; and now the papers were rolling off the machines once more.

Dermot was lying in bed at his father's hospital, to which, with a sublime disregard of red tape, Professor Wyllie had carried him off as soon as he could be moved. Hardly had he arrived when the staff nurse bustled in with a trolley and, without consulting his wishes, administered an enema. Shortly after that, she returned with a notebook in her hand and said, "Is it you that wants confession?"

"Certainly not," Dermot replied, ruffled at the bare idea.

"I have you down on me list."

"I can't help what you have on your list."

"Must be, it's the goitre next door. They're always like that before an op." She crossed something out in the book and turned to go.

"What are all those bloody bells about?" Dermot demanded, for the incessant tinkling up and down the corridor was getting on his nerves.

"Indeed, then, they're not bloody bells at all. We ring those to clear the way when a priest is coming to give patients Holy Communion or maybe anoint them."

"They make a most infernal racket, anyway. I'll need anointing myself if they keep it up much longer."

"I wouldn't wish for Sister to hear you talking like that," retorted the nurse, with a toss of her head.

Five minutes later Sister herself marched in, a squat figure with the face and air of a bulldog.

"What's this, you don't want confession?" she growled. "We have you down for it. Once you're on the list, we expect you to get it." She made it sound like massage or a dose of castor oil. "And from all I hear, you're in the want of it."

"Perhaps someone's writing isn't too good," Dermot suggested. "Could be, it's coffee they have me down for. I'd like some of that."

"Difficult patient, I see," rumbled Sister, rolling her eyes in canine fashion. "Your father told us, you should be treated like anyone else."

There was the tinkle of a bell in the passage again.

"Another moribund, I presume," said Dermot. "And no wonder, if you plague them all the way you're plaguing me. Now leave me in peace, Sister, like a dear good woman. If I want confession, I'll ring for it."

"A fine sort of Catholic!" But Sister knew she was bested and withdrew, whiffling to herself and more like a bulldog than ever.

The next visitor was an urchin of nine or so, tousled and grubby, in a torn coat several sizes too big for him, with a cigarette in his mouth and a bundle of newspapers under his arm. *"Glo-ub? Inquoirer? Toi-ums?"* he shouted, in a thick adenoidal voice, as if from a street corner.

"Is the strike over, then?" asked Dermot, sitting bolt upright in bed.

"Looks like it," the urchin said, drawing his sleeve across his dripping nose. "Unless they'd be having us on."

"Give me the *Inquirer,* so."

He did not immediately open the paper, however, but lay back on his pillows again, given up wholly to vengeful thoughts. He could cheerfully have strangled the printers, one and all, down to the last mother's son. Not content with allowing his magnificent stand to go unrecorded, they had set to work again the minute his news value disappeared altogether. It seemed an act of deliberate malice. He was no longer even in prison. Bitterly he recalled the sufferings of those first days, when his dreams, like his waking thoughts, were of nothing but food. One of those dreams had been cruelly vivid and poignant: Magee had come to him with a copy of the paper and smilingly bidden him turn to the centre pages: he had done so, expecting to see the abject apology due to him there, only to find an enormous menu, written in purple ink as in France, comprising every delicacy his famished body might crave. At this point, he awoke; and so harsh was the shock of reality after the dream, he felt that he could endure no more. His hand was actually on the bedside bell when he bethought him of the headlines next day: Crusader Ends Hunger-Strike! Wyllie Calls for Beef-Tea! and others equally humiliating; and snatching his hand away, he steeled himself to carry on. All for nothing, all in vain, no one a penny the wiser!

Now he cast a languid eye over the front page. The first piece he read filled his cup of mortification to the brim. "Brilliant new writer joins our staff," it proclaimed, with a photograph of what Dermot opined was an obvious moron beside it; and below that, after some details of the brilliant new writer, these searing words: "His first article will appear tomorrow. It is the strange story of that tormented individual who for so long has ravaged our capital and harassed our public men; who when captured and brought to justice fought his way unarmed from the court-room and was swallowed up in the teeming millions of Dublin; whose name and origins were unknown, whose hiding-place was a mystery, who came and went, driven by a sense of intolerable wrong. That man, our brilliant young colleague tracked down: that savage breast, he soothed and tamed; and from those angry lips, more used to imprecations and threats, he coaxed the whole unvarnished truth of how, more shame to us, he came to be what he is."

ORDER YOUR COPY NOW.

So this jumped-up half-wit was kicking off with a scoop! for a scoop it undoubtedly was. Not only that, but his story was billed the day before, something that had never happened to Dermot in all his year of faithful service. Wearily, he turned the pages, looking for some reference to himself, an announcement of his resignation, a tribute to his achievements, sincere good wishes for his future success. There was not a single word: Dermot Wyllie might never have been.

Then he saw another announcement to pierce him to the core. "Lovely Nuala is Back Tonight!" it said, with a picture of her embracing that bloody lamb. The television and radio people were also at work again, it seemed. Dermot felt like St Sebastian, with arrows shooting into his body from every side. His cooling-off towards her froze into an icy resolve that they should never marry. But how could he get out of it, what pretext could he find, that would satisfy public opinion and do no harm to himself? Dublin was too small, connections too interwoven, for people to act as they chose. They lived there with their sins and failures for the rest of their days.

A cup of strong black coffee was needed, to clear his brain, and he rang the bell. Presently there was a knock on the door, and a priest came in, shutting the door behind him. Having kissed his stole and arranged it round his neck, he advanced upon the bed with an encouraging smile.

"So you changed your mind! there's the good lad," he said cheerily. "Now tell me what you've been up to."

"I'm afraid there's some mistake, Father," Dermot said, glowering.

"Sister told me, if you rang, it was for confession," the priest said, with a puzzled air.

"That was only my little joke."

"It's no matter for joking, my son. While I'm here, why not take the chance? Eternity is just round the corner for us all. And you never know in this hospital—in any hospital," he corrected himself, "what may happen. Suppose now you were unlucky and got carried off? Wouldn't you look a nice fool then?"

But his pleas fell on stony ground and at last he retired, winding his stole impatiently round his fingers and much aggrieved. Dermot rang the bell again, which after twenty minutes or so was answered by the staff nurse, looking hot and cross.

"Would you ever stop ringing?" she said angrily. "It's too late for confession now."

"Does no one here ever think of anything but confession?" Dermot exploded. "Is this a madhouse?"

"No, but we have a psychiatrist. Is that what you're looking for?"

"I want a cup of strong black coffee."

"Well, then, you won't get it. You're on juices and complan. And don't be ringing that bell again, unless you're in a faint. The doctors are going their rounds, and patients make things only worse."

That night Dermot dreamed he was confessing to Nuala, who was robed as a Cardinal, and asking for ghostly counsel as to how he could avoid an unsuitable marriage.

In the morning, the front page of the *Inquirer* was just as he had feared. There were screaming headlines, a picture of the brilliant new colleague again and a royal spread. The text ran as follows:

Like the Phantom of the Opera, full of burning hate, for many months past a man has stalked through Dublin, sparing none. Leaders of public life have been subject to harassment, the like of which was never known before. They have been dragged from their beds in the small hours of the night to answer the telephone, only to hear a stream of wild abuse. They have been pelted with eggs, bottles and mud. The Dáil, Leinster House and the Four Courts have been picketed by this man, waving placards with such slogans as *Ireland is all Bastards* and *Holy Ireland, crap;* on being asked to withdraw, the man would bring his wooden placard down with a crash on the intervener's head, so that the Guards were increasingly reluctant to venture near him.

Nor did he stop at vilification. The windows of this office were smashed, as were many others, including those of a row of shops in Moore Street, now boarded up and known to the people of the locality as Little Belfast. A number of fires in pillarboxes round the city is believed to have been his handiwork as well. He was finally arrested as he made his way into the Bank of Ireland, carrying a pick-axe, with what aim in view no one can tell. But even then he was too many for the authorities. Having refused to give his name in Court or to recognize it, he fought his way out like a wild animal and was swallowed up in the teeming millions of Dublin.

MY BELIEF

After that there was a lull and people were inclined to let the matter drop. But I was not satisfied. No friend to terrorism or violence, nevertheless I told myself that men do not resort to it except in desperation. I made it my business to find this man, no matter how long or arduous the search. I roamed the streets of Dublin, by day and by night, I kept watch in places where he had been before or where he was likely to appear. No one knew him, or anything about him. All I had to go on was a photograph, somewhat blurred, of him throwing an egg at the Taoiseach.

PATIENCE REWARDED

But at last my patience was rewarded. I found him—of all places!—in Beauchamps' café, consuming a cup of tea and a buttered bun. The look of misery, despair and implacable hatred on his face was such as I never hope to see on human countenance again. I approached, not without hesitation, and asked leave to share his table. He signified his assent by jerking his head sideways, without a word. I told him I wished to help him and might be able to do so: that I was a journalist, and newspapers carried weight in this free land of ours.

MONOSYLLABLES

At first his only response was a stream of monosyllables which I will not record in these columns. But with patience, his suspicions were overcome; and after some further coaxing and wheedling, he told me his story—a grim story of man's inhumanity to man. He lived in the west, in a depressed area where there was little or no employment, and, as all his neighbours did, he depended chiefly on the dole. From time to time temporary jobs did arise, on the roads, in the ditches, collecting sand or seaweed and so forth.

HALLOWED CUSTOM

Now, it has always been the local custom, hallowed by time, to continue drawing the dole whether employed or not. Aware of the cruel struggle to live, the officer in charge had always turned a blind eye to this, even when the employed men were at work before his very windows. My friend—for so I shall call him, his name having naturally to be suppressed—at last had the good fortune to secure the post of gardener to the local parish priest: only to hear, when next he presented himself at the Labour Office, that his dole was discontinued.

DISCRIMINATION

All prayers, all representations, were in vain: he, alone in the community, was singled out for this act of discrimination. The injustice of it rankled in his mind, until he could think of nothing else. One day in the early part of last summer, when he was whitewashing the parish house, on a sudden impulse he ran with the pail to the Labour Office and dashed its contents over his tormentor's head. For this, he was dismissed from his job; and, to crown it all, when next he went to sign on for the dole, he was informed there were not sufficient stamps on his card and he must apply for help in another quarter.

But there were many others in similar case. There were those who openly bought stamps for themselves and cancelled them with the name of a fictitious employer. There were those who had never had any stamps at all.

APPEALS IN VAIN

He wrote to his T.D., none other than Ruairí na Rigg, the Minister. That gentleman replied, in a cold legalistic way, due no doubt to his English ancestry, that the law was the law and that the official concerned was merely doing his duty. Next my friend wrote to the Taoiseach, the President, the Archbishop of Dublin, the Secretary of the United Nations, Oxfam and the Council for Human Rights at Strasbourg. But all was to no purpose: he received but a polite acknowledgement of his letter or none at all.

FAILURE OF DEMOCRACY

He realized then that the democratic process had failed and that nothing was left but direct action. To this, apart from a brief spell of lifting potatoes in Scotland, he has applied himself ever since, with the results that we know. And of one thing we may be sure: until his claims are met, justice is done and blatant discrimination ended, violence will escalate here until our capital, already reeling under his blows, lies about us in ruins."

It took Dermot some time to read this stirring report, as the printers had availed themselves to the full of their recent victory. He was continually turning the paper round to get a line that was printed upside down, and there were whole sentences which appeared to be written in code. But he persevered, absorbed, oblivious of all else, unaware of staff nurse standing beside him with his complan, lost in admiration. For all his self-conceit, he was artist enough to recognize artistry, honest enough to admit he could have done no better himself. Could he, indeed, have done as well?

Sadly he shook his head. "No, no," he said, thinking aloud, and as if the words were wrung from him, "I have to confess . . . I must confess . . ."

"There now, wasn't I telling Sister that you'd come round?" cried the staff nurse in exultation. "They all do, sooner or later. Just drink that down like the grand boy and I'll have Father to you in less than five minyutes."

And without waiting for his thanks, she bustled away.

eighteen

Ever since the conversation with those vipers in the café, Grainne's secret terror had been growing. Nuala's case had been dismissed, there was no doubt of that. But cases were dismissed for all sorts of technical reasons which were no proof of innocence, true innocence, the only kind that mattered. Nuala might have been wrongfully charged with offering a contraceptive for sale, and hence acquitted. It did not mean that she had no such thing in her possession; and if she had, it could only have been for herself.

The very idea of birth control was abhorrent to Grainne Hoolahan. It was against the will of God, contrary to the laws of Holy Church and a kind of murder. That would have been enough in itself; but quite apart from the Faith, every drop of peasant blood in her body recoiled from so wasteful a practice. She had never discussed the technical side of it with anyone, and therefore had but the vaguest notion as to how it was carried out. Women took some dreadful pill, she understood, and were liable to be barren from that day forth; and a barren woman, to her, was a species of monster, good for nothing, like a barren cow or sheep.

She could not believe so horrible a thing of her child, but neither could she entirely free her mind of suspicion. And if that suspicion were founded, Nuala must be the wickedest person on earth. Nothing about her betrayed the slightest sense of doing wrong. She was gayer, happier, pleasanter to everyone and better company than ever before. If she were guilty, it could only be that she gloried in her shame.

And still the Mother of God withheld the sign that Grainne had besought of her.

Life, meanwhile, had to go on. A couple of weeks or so after the brisk exchanges with Mr. Molloy in the Dáil, Brian retired once more to St Paddy's. There were rumours of impending changes in the Government. The papers were out again and speculating freely on that likelihood. Grainne read them all with the close attention she always gave to anything that concerned the family.

"I hope they move your father to External Affairs," she said to Nuala one morning at breakfast. "He would have more to do there, to occupy his mind and keep him off the drink."

"Bracken says, they none of them do anything at all," Nuala replied, laughing.

"And what does he know about it, will you tell me?"

"Ah, Bracken gets around."

Here they were interrupted by the drudge, who made up the entire staff of Capri Heights now that Geraldine had left. She came slouching in with the early post, in which, to Grainne's surprise and delight, was a civil note from Lady Belling. As if the unpleasantness between them had never occurred, she informed Grainne that Summers had applied to her for domestic employment, and that she would be glad to hear if Mrs Hoolahan would furnish a reference.

"Fancing her calling Geraldine 'Summers'!" Grainne marvelled. "I would never have dared."

"I shouldn't answer if I were you," was Nuala's advice. "She'll find out fast enough what Geraldine's like, and then it'll come back on yourself."

But the prospect of forging a link between Castle Trig and Capri Heights at last quite carried Grainne away.

"I'll have to say what I can for the poor woman," she replied happily. "And the things about her that annoyed me most, her puffing at cigarettes and her sauce, Lady Belling will be able for. She'll not get a walk-over there. I'll knock something reasonable out."

What she knocked out was pretty effusive and stretched a great many points, among them, even, that she regretted having to let Summers go but that she was at present over-staffed. A few days later Geraldine herself swaggered up to the front-door in her Sunday best, graciously thanked Mrs Hoolahan for her good opinion and notified her that she was to start with her ladyship in the morning.

"I always wanted to work for gentry," she confided, as she took a stately departure.

The morrow, however, brought one of those cruel anti-climaxes that constantly fell to Grainne's lot. She was sitting in the drawing-room by the window, wondering how much time must elapse before she could decently ring up the Castle to inquire after the new servant's conduct, when Geraldine herself came toiling up the drive. She was pushing a wheelbarrow laden with junk, old lampshades, sauce-pans, an eiderdown, a battered suitcase, a broken chair, an umbrella, a greasy overcoat and a huge feathery fan. When Grainne hurried out to ask the meaning of it, she at once recognized each item as a possession of her own, long discarded. Too winded to answer her horrified questions, Geraldine merely handed over an envelope, containing another of the 'From: Maude, Lady Belling' cards with the message: "Lady Belling presents her compliments and begs to say she cannot allow her grounds to be used as the Capri Heights' dump. Mrs Hoolahan will doubtless be pleased to hear, however, that Summers is once more available, should her services be required."

"Twas all that dustman, the divil fly off with him," panted Geraldine, on the verge of tears. "He wouldn't take nothing away but what fitted into the bin. So what could I do, only sling the lot over the wall, into her ladyship's spinney, where they'd be no obstruction? But that gardener she has is worse than a bloodhound. And her ladyship never meant to engage me at all," poor Geraldine went on, completely breaking down. "It was just her idea of a joke, the hoor!"

"And what was wrong with your head, that you couldn't tell me about the dustman?" Grainne demanded, raging. "He only wanted a tip."

"I meant it for the best, like I always do," Geraldine sobbed. "The way that woman spoke to me, it shouldn't happen a dog. If the IRA knew the half, they'd surely burn her out."

Thus one more social tentative had ended in disaster.

"Why bother with such people, Mummy?" Nuala asked, when she heard the news later on. "Bracken says, they're only laughing at us up their sleeve. He says, their nose is out of joint and all that's left them is to sneer."

"What could I do, when she wanted the reference, the dirty double-crosser?" asked Grainne bitterly. "She'd a right to be mad, fair play for her, with Geraldine heaving that stuff across. But to take such a wicked revenge! I'm through with the upper classes!"

"Well, that's one mercy, anyhow." But Nuala spoke kindly, and was so attentive and charming all day, that presently the wound began to heal.

It was not too long, however, before a fresh and darker cloud was looming on the horizon. Grainne came of a large family, all of whom, save one, were married and living in England or America. The exception was a sister who, following the custom of rural Ireland, had sacrificed herself to stay at home and mind the parents as they grew old. For doing this, again according to custom, she would in due course inherit all they had to leave. The mother had died many years before, the father was on the brink of dotage, and the sister's release seemed not too far away.

Grainne had always taken it for granted that when this happened, she must give, or at any rate offer, her sister a home. She did not look forward to this graceless addition to the household, but family was family. But now, contrary to all expectation and precedent, the sister it was who suddenly upped and died or—as the father's telegram put it—'passed on.' There was nothing for it but to take him in instead, a crude old man of dreadful habits and a voice like a foghorn, deaf, with the deaf person's insistence that every little remark be shouted over and over until he finally grasped it. Among other points that told against him was, that he seldom bothered to fasten his flies and, at meal times, took his teeth out and rested them on the table, mumbling his food with his gums and only replacing the teeth when he had finished. Nor was he one to be left out of anything going: there could be no question of a tray upstairs when Grainne had guests to dinner, or of an early bed-time when the Hoolahans were invited out themselves. The future looked almost too dire for contemplation, and Grainne was half disposed to believe that here at last was that sign from the Mother of God, signifying all-round displeasure.

"But must you really have him here?" Nuala asked, knowing how much her mother disliked him, apart from his repulsive ways. "Would he not be as well in a home? There's a great one down in Dalkey, and you could visit him every day. Bracken says, old people are happiest in company with the old."

"Does he so!" exclaimed Grainne hotly. "Well, let him. Put your grandfather in a home! I could never hold up my head again. He's a right to come here and that's all about it. We must put up with him the best we can."

Nuala did not argue the point, her mind being full of more engrossing matters. "When's the funeral to be?" she asked, in a distant kind of way, as if it did not really concern her.

"As soon as the family get here," said her mother. "I'll have to start 'phoning England at once and cabling America. The Yanks will hardly come, I'd say. Queer, how they fall off, when they get over there. And I'll have to alert your brothers and sisters, Grandpa left everything to me. There's no end to be done, God only knows where everyone's going to sleep. We'll have to go down the minute I have the messages sent."

"We? You don't mean I should come?" Nuala exclaimed.

"To the funeral, Nuala? I most certainly do."

"But I hardly knew Aunt Connie. In fact, I didn't know her at all."

This was true. She had only seen the woman once or twice, as a very small child, and if the house were not so rife with family photographs would hardly have known how she looked.

"What's that to do with it?" Grainne demanded, staring

at her. "My sister! Your aunt! Isn't it shocking enough, that your father won't be there?"

God help us, the family and its tentacles . . .

"Then I'll come on after by the train," Nuala said, with all her sullenness back, just as ever, as if it had merely been folded away in a drawer. "There's something I have to do first. I was on my way to it when the telegram came."

"Something you have to do first!" Grainne cried. "I'll have a thousand things to do, and I'm looking to you to help me. You don't know what a death in the country is, Nuala. You were too young to bring when Granny died. It's not only the Mass and the funeral, although God knows they're bad enough. But it's entertaining the neighbours, talking and talking half the night through, and getting it all together, and finding beds for the family, and I don't know what. Someone will have laid her out, but there's no habit or coffin ordered, you may be sure. And after that, there'll be the house to close and your grandfather to pack for. What you have to do can't be as urgent as this. Just ring up and say there's a sudden death in the family. That ought to be sufficient for any Christian."

"Oh death death death," said Nuala impatiently. "What a fuss people make of it!"

"It's the most important thing in life," Grainne affirmed, with solemnity. "Will you not come with me, childeen? Ah, do. I declare, I'm moidered already, just with the thinking."

But Nuala was obdurate. Prayers and entreaties failed to move her. She promised to try and come on the evening train or, if that were impossible, by the early one in the morning. With that, she pulled on her helmet and strode off to the Yamaha.

Wearily, Grainne set about her duties alone. She sent off the cables to America first and got them out of the way. Next she began the more arduous work of ringing up Maureen in London, Eddie in Manchester and Tomo in Liverpool. On such an occasion decency required that she talk to them at some length, with no appearance of hurry: it ate up the precious time but there was no way round it. All expressed the sorrow that decency required of *them,* and said they would travel at once. Her own children were easier to manage, as she simply rang Fr Matt and asked him to tell the others.

"It's terrible news, all right," said Fr Matt, unable to keep the irritation out of his voice. "I'll be saying the Mass, I suppose?"

"Ah, you'll talk to the priest down there about it."

And a proper old bison Fr Mulcahy was: Grainne could see the battle ahead. But for the present all she need do was get out her mourning clothes, which she kept always fresh and tidy as a kind of insurance against their being called for, pack, give various instructions to the drudge, well knowing she would disregard them, and at last drive away.

A new housing estate with a forest of TV aerials had sprung up on the edge of the city since Grainne had last taken that road. Once it was left behind, it was like going from one world to another. The country seemed all but deserted: for mile after mile there was hardly a soul about. The sky was grey, and an afternoon mist was creeping up, making the autumn colours of hedge and tree glow all the more brightly. She raced on past the empty fields and through the familiar dull little towns until she came to the one, exactly like all the rest, which had been her birthplace.

On reaching it, as often happened, she found that nothing was as bad as she had expected. Black Biddy, one of those kind-hearted ghouls that haunt the Irish country scene, on hearing of Connie's death had immediately made her way to the house and taken charge. All was scrubbed, polished and dusted, and rows of teapots, cups and saucers and plates were ready assembled. Connie lay decently on the bed, her hands, clasping a rosary, resting on the coverlet: she looked smaller than when she was living, but her features wore their everyday expression, melancholy and resigned. Black Biddy had even got the door removed to make room for the coffin bearers: long practice in this field had made her perfect. Sister Dolours, arriving sooner than Grainne, had ordered the coffin and habit and now was running to and fro in search of beds for those who could not be squeezed under the ancestral roof. Fr Matt was also here, and had gone to call on the parish priest. Grainne began to feel that she no longer carried the weight of the world alone.

The reaction of her father was unexpected too. She had thought to find him dazed, at sea, helpless as a lame man whose crutches are taken away: instead he was bubbling over with merriment and a weird sort of triumph. Neighbours who called to express their regret for the death were surprised to be greeted with noisy bursts of laughter; and he chuckled incessantly as he sat by himself in the parlour. Black Biddy had persuaded him to put on his Sunday suit and to remove his cap, which he was wont never to do except at Mass or in bed; and a strange figure he was, his bald skull and upper forehead of a sepulchral pallor, the rest of his face and his neck a fiery crimson, as he cackled and crowed and wiped the tears of mirth from his eyes.

"Who'da t'ought it? Who'da t'ought it?" they heard him mutter, as they went about their tasks in the kitchen.

"It's been too much for the father, the shock at his age," Grainne whispered to Black Biddy. In her childhood home she was falling easily into the old ways of speech: at Capri Heights, before she referred to him as 'the father' she would have bitten her tongue out.

"Ah, he'll settle after a bit, please God," Black Biddy

comforted her. "If we can only get him through the funeral without any incidents."

Fr Matt returned from his confrontation with Fr Mulcahy with the joyful news that he was to say the requiem Mass. There had been a struggle all right, but this had ended with a gentleman's agreement about the Mass cards. The proceeds were to be split fifty-fifty: Grainne thought it foolishly generous, even quixotic, but realized that a cut-and-thrust haggle would have been out of place.

One by one throughout the evening her other children joined them, Caitlin, Edward FitzGerald and finally Liam. Only Nuala was missing when, after the hours of hushed but friendly talk with old friends and neighbours, at last they got to bed. In the morning, Tomo, Maureen and Eddie arrived from England, and still there was no Nuala. But Grainne was so absorbed and her mind so strangely at peace that she scarcely gave the child a thought. It was good to be here, after all, where she really belonged, where nobody sneered or snubbed, where on the contrary all respected her, were proud that she had risen above themselves, yet looked on her as one of their own and were simple and cordial in their manner towards her.

As Black Biddy had prophesied, her father quietened after a while and they got through the various rituals without disgrace. Only when these were over did he burst uncontrollably forth again, and since none but the family and the lawyer were present to hear him, it was of no great consequence. Poor Connie, the creature, methodical as always, had left a will and drawn it up in the natural expectation that her father would die before herself. She had accordingly disposed of all the property, still his, that should have come to her: the house, the store, the little bit of land, were to be sold and the monies accruing from them, together with all other assets in cash, were to be divided equally between the local parish priest, whoever he might be at the relevant time, and the local convent.

When the embarrassed lawyer read this out, the wicked old fellow laughed like a madman.

"Ah, Connie, Connie," he spluttered. "Wasn't I wan too many for yeh? Wasn't I now? Wan too many!"

There was no stopping him at all and, to make an awkward moment worse, Edward FitzGerald joined in.

"I had no idea the woman was so religious," was the acid comment of Fr Matt, later, as he was preparing to leave. "And to think of her, leaving it away from her own!"

"Ah now, Matt, when it wasn't hers to leave," Edward FitzGerald, smiling broadly, consoled him.

Until the last formality was concluded, Grainne had not cared to raise the question of her father's home. She did so now, assuring him with all the warmth she could summon up, that he was welcome to make it with her. To her great surprise and still greater relief, he flatly refused to budge from the hearth and home where he had always lived and firmly intended to die.

"I'll stay where I'm boss," he told her. "With respects to yeh."

"But who's going to tend you, da?" Grainne objected, although her heart grew light within her.

"Arrah, I'll tind to meself," he snapped. "If I don't get married again! I might do it yet, and rear a new family too, the way ye'll all be amazed."

There had never been any arguing with the man. A great black cloud had rolled away. When all the farewells had been said and Grainne began the drive home, she found herself actually singing at the wheel. But then all at once she thought of Nuala, and the song died on her lips. A cloud had rolled away, to be sure, but another was ready to take its place, as always and then no doubt another and another, in steady procession.

nineteen

"The Monsignor is here, Professor," said Mollie, the chief assistant. She had noiselessly opened the consulting-room door and noiselessly shut it behind her. "Shall I put him in ahead of the other patients?"

"Indeed you will not," said Professor Wyllie, buttoning up his white jacket. "I'm not going to see the bloody old fool at all. He never does as he's told."

To hear the higher clergy spoken of in this way was one of the pleasures of working at the clinic.

"What'll I tell him?"

"Whatever you like. Is there a crowd out there? We'd

better get going, the hospital wants me as soon as I've done."

"There's a crowd all right. And Nuala Hoolahan is here, urgently wants to see you," Mollie said. "I told her, you were rushed off your feet, but she said she couldn't help that."

The Professor put his stethescope round his neck and sat down at the writing-table, with a glance at the crowded appointment-book. "Send her in," he said briefly. "Now."

"But she isn't a patient, Professor," Mollie demurred. "She's not on the list. It's something private."

"I decide who's a patient or isn't," Professor Wyllie proclaimed. "And if she's engaged to my son, she is. An honorary patient, anyhow. Don't make out a card."

Mollie left as silently as she had come, and after an interval reappeared with Nuala, who was very pale and, at the sight of the Professor, known to her only from Dermot's description, grew paler still.

"Sit down, m'dear, and relax," he commanded, taking this in. "Now, Moll, what is it?" For Moll was hovering, evidently with something to say.

"The Monsignor," she murmured, "is cutting up rough."

The Professor rose and marched out of the room, returning in less than a minute. "He's gone," he announced. "You must learn to talk to them, Moll. Now don't let anyone in and don't put any calls through.

"Well, Nuala, it's time we were acquainted, isn't it?" he went on, seating himself again, and talking in another, gentler voice. "Tell me what the trouble is. Take your time, but come to the point at once, or the crowd out there will lynch me. Good heavens, the child is trembling! I suppose Dermot told you his father's a dragon."

'Dragon' was mild indeed, compared to the terms employed by that filial youth.

197

"I don't know what to do," faltered Nuala. "I can't get in touch with him. It took me ages to find him even, he'd left the newspaper and the flat . . . Well never mind, I mustn't delay you. When I got to the hospital where he is, they told me he was seeing no visitors. I said, I was his fiancée, and they went off to ask him, but came back with the same reply. So I sat down then and there and wrote him a letter, and asked them to give it him. They said they would, but not at once, he was making his confession just then. I never knew him confessing before."

"Nor I," said his father, with the ghost of a grin.

"And it seemed to go on for hours."

"I can imagine it might."

"At long last they came back and said there was no answer. I couldn't believe it, it was so frightfully important. I told them, see him I would, but they wouldn't hear of it, wouldn't give me the number of his room. He seems to have them all in his pocket."

"He has. The one thing he's good at," the Professor remarked drily. "When was all this?"

"The day before yesterday. I thought there might be something in the post since then, but no, nothing." Nuala broke down suddenly and wept. "I don't know what to do, I don't know what to do," she sobbed.

The Professor leaned forward and put one of his hands on hers. "Now now now," he said kindly. "Nuala, my dear, are you certain you want to marry that boy of mine? He'll never make a husband. I don't want to hurt you, but truth is always best. You are not the first—by a long chalk, not the first."

Nuala looked up at him through her tears, wonderingly, like a child. "Not the first?" she echoed.

Professor Wyllie shook his head.

At this there was a fresh downpour. "It doesn't make

any difference," Nuala wept. "We *must* get married. At once!"

The Professor so far forgot his dignity as to give a long low whistle.

"So that's how it is!" he exclaimed. "You poor wee thing. You poor wee thing. Are you absolutely sure?"

"Absolutely. There's no doubt in the world."

"Does your mother know?"

"Not yet. But she will have to soon. She's in the country now, at her sister's funeral." Nuala pulled her self together and dried her tears. Having come all braced to tackle a fiend in human form, she had met with nothing but kindness and sympathy, no contempt, no censure, no hint that she was a fallen women with only herself to thank for it; and she found her courage returning. "She was wild that I didn't go with her," she continued, trying to smile. "I told her, I had something important to do, and she said, death was the most important thing in life!"

"God help us!" the Professor exploded. "We doctors are wasting our time, then, aren't we?" Pious mother, drunken father, used and thrown away by my precious son, he thought: the poor wee scrap. "Would you like me to tell her for you?"

"Ah no, you're very good but I'll have to do it. Only, it'll kill her all right, unless I can say we're to marry." Nuala looked at him with a pleading expression. "I thought, maybe, you could talk to Dermot."

"I could talk to Dermot all right," his father agreed, bitterly. "And I will, if you wish it. But I'd be using my breath as well, haranguing the table between us. He has only to hear something from me, to go the opposite way. And I've no stick to beat him with. He's of age. I could cut him off with a shilling, but his mother has money, and she'd refuse him nothing. That's the one he's married to, and always will be. Think about this, Nuala. Do you seriously intend to marry a man, here in Ireland where there's no divorcing, who'd make a rotten husband, and a father—if possible—worse?"

"Sure, what else can I do?"

"You could go to England, for instance, where they see things differently, have the child, get it adopted or keep it as you prefer. That's something I could help you with, send you to good friends of mine, stand by you from start to finish, give you whatever you need." He smiled at her. "That's my grandchild you have there, remember."

"It's wonderful of you, just wonderful," Nuala stammered. "But please, I'd rather you spoke to Dermot. You could perhaps find out what's the matter, at least? I can't make head or tail of it. We haven't even quarrelled, not really. It's true, when I started on TE I was too busy to see him as often as usual, but he ought to understand that. I don't know how many times he's dropped *me* at the last minute, if there was something he had to do for the paper. I've sat by the hour, waiting somewhere, and he never even sent word. And he didn't like what I did on TE, said it was corny and cheap."

The Professor knew well that immediately after Nuala's leap to fame Dermot had bragged of her all over town, as to some extent it rubbed off on himself; but he allowed this to pass without comment.

"But that was only a disagreement," Nuala went on. "There was never a word from him, about actually wanting to break things off. Why, almost the last time I saw him before he disappeared, he asked me for twenty-five pounds! Would he have done that, if he didn't consider us still engaged?"

At this the Professor laughed outright, a rare occurrence with him: a couple of times a year was the average.

"I can see you're hopeless," he remarked. "Well, I'll talk to the villain this very night. But if I don't succeed—as I won't—will you think about the suggestion I made?"

"No, I'll have to stick it out," Nuala sighed, despondent once more, feeling the invisible chains about her. "There's no escape. It must be, this is the punishment for my sin."

"Bah! punishment for your sin!" the Professor growled. "Nuns' claptrap. A baby is the natural consequence of making love."

Nuala hung her head, blushing to the roots of her hair. "That's just it, that's the sin I meant," she said, almost in a whisper. "We . . . we used things . . . you know . . . those things that everyone's on about . . . And it must be, one of them didn't work. If that isn't a punishment from God, I wonder what else it could be?"

This interpretation of life merely confirmed the Professor in his opinion that Ireland was lunatic to the core.

"Well, away with you now, before those people out there have me in pieces," he said, rising to his feet. "You're alone in the house at present? Good, I'll ring you this evening after I've talked to my son. But don't expect much, and remember, whatever happens, you've got me to turn to."

With that, having uttered more words than he usually did in the course of a day, he showed her out; and she rode off to Capri Heights, feeling, in spite of God's anger, a little less forlorn and distracted.

Professor Wyllie was a man difficult to surprise; and he himself would have told you that where his son was concerned, it could not be done. Dermot's engagement to Nuala, which sent his mother into near-hysterics, puzzled him not at all, following as it did upon Brian's promotion to Minister; and now that Brian was on the way out, to break with her was clearly the boy's next step. That he would also leave her in the lurch, if lurch arose, was likewise a foregone conclusion.

Then there was the state of affairs at the hospital. Here, the Professor was a kind of deity, expecting and receiving compliance with all his wishes. He had laid it down that Dermot was not to be pampered or made much of, but restored to health, briskly and unsympathetically, as soon as might be, to stand his trial. Matron had promised this should be done, and instructed the Sister in charge, who passed the order on to the nurses involved; and now the lot of them, Matron and all, were eating out of Dermot's hand, spoiling him to death, buying him flowers and running his errands. They fondly imagined that Professor did not know: he did, but held his peace. The news that Dermot was shriving himself, which would have amazed and overjoyed his mother, merely tickled the male parent. It had been done, as all that the boy did was, with some ulterior motive, the most probable being, to ingratiate himself still further with the hospital staff, which, in the Professor's view, was rotten with piety.

When therefore, true to his promise, he went to the hospital to reason with the culprit, it was in the belief that he knew more or less how the discussion would go. Dermot would say that they were too young to know their own minds, that they had made a mistake and it was better to realize it now, when they could still draw back: or he would dwell with pathos on his lack of a job, his want of means, and the possibility of his going to prison: or, again, he might simply refuse to talk about it at all. But what in fact he put forward as the excuse was such as not merely to astound his father, but positively, to take his breath away.

He heard the Professor out, with a gentle courteous patience that was foreign to his usual manner, and yet, at the same time, with some little air of not being able to believe his ears. Then he was silent awhile, communing with himself, as one who seeks a tactful reply to a suggestion wholly preposterous.

"Do I understand you, Father?" he asked at length. "Are you saying I should marry Nuala Hoolahan?"

"Of course I am," the Professor said, glowering. At the mere sight of the boy, his choler had risen. "It's your duty."

"But how could I do such a thing? How could I bring her into the family?" Dermot wished to know. "She's an unchaste woman!"

It was here that the Professor, momentarily, was deprived of speech.

"How could Mummy be expected to receive her as a daughter?" the holy youth went on, in unctuous tones that he never had used before. "Feeling as she does about such matters? It might be the death of her. Ask her yourself, and see what she says."

"Leave your mother out of it," gasped the Professor, having swallowed hard a few times. "Nuala is carrying your child . . ."

"If it *is* my child," Dermot broke in, raising a finger in monitory fashion.

"You young blackguard!"

"I don't see it like that, Father. A man has the right to be sure that the children he rears are his own. And once a woman has fallen, the probability is, she will fall again. Ask Mummy if that isn't so."

"You young blackguard," repeated the Professor, his speech now fully restored. "So that's what all this confessing was about! How did I ever breed such vermin?" he demanded, staring wildly round the room as if in the hope that someone would tell him. "What have I done to deserve it?"

"I'm sorry that you feel so strongly," Dermot said with

composure, rising above the vulgar abuse. "But I'm convinced that, when you think about it calmly, you'll see that I'm right."

The Professor flung out of the room without more ado.

Later, he rang Nuala up. "It's as I thought, my dear," he said. "Nothing to be done. I have put a letter in the post to Mrs Hoolahan, under cover to you. When you have told her the story, please see that she gets it."

How *did* I ever breed such vermin? he kept wondering through that night, with Mrs Wyllie snoring beside him and Nuala's sobs still echoing in his ears.

twenty

In the morning Nuala went to rehearsal, and afterwards lunched with Bracken, as by now was their regular habit. There was nothing for it but to tell him the truth. Anxiously scrutinizing herself in the full-length mirror, she had been aware of a change in her outline, and shortly it must become apparent to all. It was neither painful nor embarrassing to reveal everything to this man, for she had grown extremely fond of him and felt that he was of her. Indeed, at the back of her mind there was some vague hope that he would marry her himself. Perhaps it was her youth that prompted this, the part of her still a child that was half-disposed to believe in fairyland and Father Christmas; or perhaps it was sheer desperation. At all events, the thought was there; and the shocked concern she saw in his face when he heard the news seemed to show that, at least, he was not indifferent to what befell her.

"Oh Janey Mack!" he said, running his hands through his hair as he always did when a thorny problem cropped up. "If this isn't the divil's own luck! What on earth's to be done?"

He sat there frowning, lost in thought, for a longish while, with Nuala hardly able to breathe.

Then suddenly, "I've got it!" he exclaimed in triumph. "All we do is, change the story, break away from convention. Why should a marriage always come at the end? We'll have it now, so that your poor ailing mammy—we'll have to step her illness up—can see it before she dies. That'll be ground enough for the sudden decision. And we'll carry on from there, with simple natural family life, such as never was screened before!"

"But what about me?" quavered poor Nuala. "How can I go through with it? An unmarried mother!"

"Oh, that," said the producer absently, his mind on the complex adjustments to be made in the script. "Not to worry. Everyone knows you're engaged to Dermot. Put on a ring and say you married him quietly. He'll skip to England as soon as he's well, to avoid the court proceedings, so he won't be here to deny it. You can say your parents didn't approve, but you couldn't let him down."

And with this chilly comfort Nuala had to be content. Her last faint hope extinguished, she went home to await her mother's return in a condition approaching despair. She realized now that the appreciative, understanding Bracken had, all along, thought only of his programme and the use she could be to it, in other words, of himself. But wasn't she just the same, wasn't she thinking only of herself? Wasn't everyone the same? It was a wonder the world jogged on at all, with millions and millions of people centred on themselves, bothering about no one else . . .

The telephone rang: it was Grainne.

"Ah, you're in," she said. "I called before, but there was no reply. I'm at Longford now, won't be long getting home. I thought I'd let you know, your grandfather isn't coming. I did my best to persuade him, but he wouldn't hear of leaving the country. The neighbours are going to keep an eye on things, God be good to them! So there's a worry that's out of the way."

Deep in her trouble, Nuala had quite forgotten the nasty old man. As she put the receiver down, she felt a sudden tender warmth for her mother. With all the silliness, the snobbery, the vulgar ways of talking and behaving, here was one who did think of others, did carry out her duty to them. That remark she had dropped one day, talking about birth control, how was it?—'If your father and I had done as you seem to think we should, you might have been left out of it too'?—came all at once to Nuala's mind, and for the first time in her life she saw how fundamentally good a woman Grainne Hoolahan was. And now she had to break her heart. It was agonizing. What should she say? How could she tell her? She mentally framed one little careful speech after another, and rejected them all.

Grainne arrived, laden with fresh country eggs and butter and home-baked loaves that the neighbours had heaped upon her. Having deposited these in the kitchen, she sank onto the drawing-room sofa and kicked off her shoes.

"So you didn't make it," she said unresentfully. "No harm, everything went off better than I thought it would. But what's wrong with you, childeen? You're as pale as a ghost. Were you starving yourself again? Amn't I always telling you, you've a lovely figure, and not a single ounce too many?"

Nuala went across to her and knelt down at her side.

"Dermot doesn't want to marry me, Mummy," she said, with a catch in her voice.

"Does he not? So that's the trouble. Well, he never was good enough for you," Grainne said, stroking her hair. "And does it grieve you, darling? It must, of course, for a while. But you're very young, and all of life's before you."

"Mummy . . . Mummy . . ." Nuala was almost unable to speak for the lump in her throat. "Can you forgive me? I'm going to have a baby." And, trembling, she bowed before whatever should come, cries of horror, reproaches angry, bitter or sorrowful, curses perhaps, even a wish to see her dead.

To her stupefaction, there was nothing of the kind. Her mother's face lit up and she drew a long deep breath, as if some intolerable weight were suddenly lifted from her.

"My little love! My little precious lamb!" she cried, drawing Nuala to her and kissing her passionately. "I knew, I always knew in my heart that you were sound! It was all those wicked gossiping women and those stupid police. Forgive you! It's myself should be on my own two knees this minute, asking your forgiveness and thanking the Blessed Virgin! Let this be a lesson to me, never to mind what people say again!"

"But Mummy!" gasped the bewildered mother-to-be. "I haven't a husband!"

"Sure, what harm?" said Grainne happily. "You're not the first and you'll not be the last. We'll face it out together."

"But what will all of them say to it? Matt? Dolours? Daddy?"

"Is it Matt?" demanded Grainne, the lioness in her fully aroused. "He'll say, 'I told you so,' and as long as he can say that, he'll be satisfied. And if Joola opens her mouth at all, I'll quench her. Just for she's married to Jesus Christ, she needn't go thinking she's someone. And you can leave your father to me. It's my belief, he'll be only delighted. He was fit to be tied when they brought that summons here. The shocking, despicable injustice of it! I hope they all feel ashamed of themselves, when the news gets about. There's Dublin for you, nothing but slander and spite, and a great old fool is Dublin going to look!"

Helplessly, Nuala began to laugh. Grainne prattled away, full of plans for the baby and a pilgrimage to Knock, for Brian to leave politics, where he'd never done a moment's good since he mixed himself up in them, but they'd have to give him a Minister's pension, and to go back to the business, which had grown too much for Liam alone, and they'd all live in the country where you had decent good neighbours, not aristocrats with English accents; she was fairly spilling over, and only interrupted herself now and then to shower kisses on that blameless poor victim of evil tongues.

"This is the best thing to happen for ages," she declared, when at last she'd talked herself out. "And we'll have a baby in the house, what's more. A home isn't a home without one. And as for husbands, don't mind them. What are they, only flies in the ointment?"

"There's a letter for you from Dermot's father," Nuala said shyly, proffering it. "I went to see him, and he was angelic."

Professor Wyllie had written briefly and to the point.

"No use my telling you how sorry and ashamed I am, you'll realize that," the letter ran. "I simply want you to know that, until someone better qualified comes along, I shall consider myself as Nuala's father-in-law. I look forward to seeing my grandchild. Whatever I can do to help, shall be done."

"There's the Quality for you," Grainne purred. "The

real Quality, none of your jumped-up Johnnies. And now I'm going to wet the tea, all the excitement has me parched."

She bustled off to the kitchen. Wide-eyed, Nuala watched her go, half thinking it must be a dream: then she broke into helpless laughter again, on and on and on.

About the Author

HONOR TRACY is English by birth, Irish by residence. Her reputation as one of the leading satirical novelists of the day was firmly established with her first novel, *The Straight and Narrow Path*. She has published five books of nonfiction, most recently *Winter in Castille,* and nine novels, all of which have received critical acclaim on both sides of the Atlantic. She lives in County Mayo, Ireland.